'Exhilarating... Cook's is a fresh and vivid voice; it's unsurprising the likes of Miranda July and Roxane Gay are fans.'   *Observer*

'A deeply original collection...deliciously unsettling...uncomfortably resonant.'   *Independent*

'Makes for compulsive reading... Chilling and darkly comic.'
          New Statesman

'Sharply written and imaginative... Brilliant.'   *Irish Times*

'*Man V. Nature* is a knockout...every single story could make a great movie.'   Miranda July, *New York Times*

'Lively, apocalypse-tinged tales... Cook mines the moments that precede the losses—when the battles are truly raging—and it's in them that she finds great beauty and strangeness... And, in the end, this collection suggests, meaning might be worth the battle.'
          New York Times Book Review

'Astonishing...the stories are surreal, with the sharpest edge and in one way or another, each story reveals something raw and powerful about being human in a world where so little is in our control.'
          Roxane Gay, author of *Bad Feminist*

'*Man V. Nature* is as close to experiencing a Picasso as literature can get: the worlds in Diane Cook's impressive debut are bizarre, vertiginous, funny, pushed to the extreme—but just familiar enough in their nuances of the human condition to evoke an irresistible, around-the-corner reality.'
          Téa Obreht, author of *The Tiger's Wife*

'Here's a good rule: If Diane Cook wrote it, read it... Safety is tenuous, if not an illusion, in her thoughtful, unsettling, and darkly funny collection.'   *Boston Globe*

'These are grir   d-r-k but dizzyingly alive.'
          ry Express

MAN v. NATURE

DIANE COOK

ONEWORLD

A Oneworld Book

First published in the United Kingdom and Australia
by Oneworld Publications, 2015
This edition published 2020

ISBN 978-1-78607-885-8
ISBN 978-1-78074-816-0 (eBook)

Versions of the following stories have been previously published:
"Moving On" in *Tin House*
"The Way the End of Days Should Be" (as "Bounty") in *Harper's Magazine*
"Somebody's Baby" in *Salt Hill Journal*
"Marrying Up" in *Guernica*
"Flotsam" in *Redivider*
"The Mast Year" in *Granta*
"The Not-Needed Forest" in *Zoetrope: All-Story*

Designed by Sunil Manchikanti
Printed and bound in Great Britain by Clays Ltd, Elcograf S.p.A.

Oneworld Publications
10 Bloomsbury Street
London WC1B 3SR
England

Stay up to date with the latest books,
special offers, and exclusive content from
Oneworld with our newsletter

Sign up on our website
oneworld-publications.com

MIX
Paper from
responsible sources
FSC
www.fsc.org   FSC® C018072

FOR MY MOM

The Wilderness is new—to you.

Master, let me lead you.

EMILY DICKINSON

CONTENTS

MOVING ON

They let me tend to my husband's burial and settle his affairs, which means that for a few days I get to stay in my house, pretend he is away on business while I stand in the closet and smell his clothes. I cook dinners for two and throw the rest away, or overeat, depending on my mood. I make a time capsule of pictures I won't be allowed to keep. I bury it in the yard for a new family to discover.

But once that work is done, the Placement Team orders me to pack two bags of essentials, good for any climate. They take the keys to our house, our car. A crew will come in, price it all, and a sale will be advertised; all the neighbors will come. I won't be here for any of this, but I've seen it happen to others. The money will go into my dowry, and then someday, hopefully, another man will marry me.

I have a good shot at getting chosen, since I'm a good decorator and we have some pretty nice stuff to sell off and so my dowry will likely be enticing. And the car is pretty new, and in the last year I was the only one who could drive it and I kept it clean. It's a nice car with leather seats and lots of extras. It was my husband's promotion gift to himself, though he drove it for only a few months before illness swept him into his bed. It's also a big family car, which will appeal to the neighbors, who all have big families. We hadn't started our own yet. We were fretting over money, being practical. I'm lucky we didn't. Burdened women are more difficult to place, I'm told. They separate mothers from children. I've heard it can be very hard on everyone. The children are like phantom limbs that ache on a mother's body. I wouldn't know, but I'm good at imagining.

They drive me away from our house, and I see all the leaves that fell while I was too busy burying my husband and worrying what would become of me. The leaves, glossy and red, pile in circles around the tree trunks like Christmas-tree skirts. I see the rake propped against the rainspout. The least I could have done is rake the yard one last time. I told my husband I would.

o o o

I am taken to a women's shelter on a road that leads out to the interstate. They don't let us go beyond the compound's fence, because the land is ragged and wild. The night skies are overwhelmed with stars, and animals howl far off. Sometimes hiding men ambush the women scurrying from the bus to the gate, and the guards, women themselves, don't always intervene. Sometimes they even help. As with all things, there is a black market for left-behind women, most often widowed, though in rare cases irreconcilable differences can land one in a shelter. A men's shelter is across the road. It is smaller, and mainly for widowers who are poor or who cannot look after themselves. My father ended up in one of these shelters in Florida. A wealthy woman who had put her career first chose him. Older now, she wanted a mate. They sent him to her, somewhere in Texas. I lost track of him. The nearest children's shelter is in a different county.

My room has a sealed window that faces the road, and when I turn off my light I can see men like black stars in their bright rooms. I watch them move in their small spaces. I wonder what my new husband will be like.

o o o

There are so many handouts and packets. We have been given schedules and rules and also suggestions for improving our lives and looks. It's like a spa facility on lockdown. We are encouraged to take cooking classes, sewing classes, knitting classes, gardening classes, conceiving classes, body-bounce-back-from-pregnancy classes, child-rearing classes, feminine-assertiveness classes, jogging classes, nutrition classes, home economics. There are bedroom-technique potlucks and mandatory "Moving On" seminars.

In my first "Moving On for Widows" seminar we are given a manual of helpful exercises and visualizations. For one, I'm to remember seeing my husband for the first time—we met at a new hires lunch—and then imagine the moment happening differently. So, for example, rather than sitting next to him and knocking his water onto his welcome packet, I should visualize walking right by him and sitting alone. Or, if I let myself sit down and spill his water, instead of him laughing and our hands tangling in the nervous cleanup, I should picture him yelling at me for my clumsiness. I'm supposed to pretend our wedding day was lonely and that rather than feeling love and happiness, I felt doubt, dread. It's all very hard.

But, they say, it's helpful in getting placed. What I find funny is that since my husband died—as he was dying, really—I hadn't considered that this might be hard. I thought it was just the next step. My Case Manager says that this is normal, and that the feeling of detachment comes from shock. She says that if I can hold on to it and skip over the bewildering grief that follows, I'll be better off. The grief-stricken spend more time here. Years, in some cases. "Practice, practice, practice," she always says.

We're each given a framed picture of a man, some model, and I take it back to my cell and put it by my bed as instructed. I'm supposed to replace my husband's face in my memory with this man's face while being careful not to get too attached; the man in the photo won't be my new husband. The man is too smooth; his teeth are very straight and white, and there is a glistening in his hair from gel that has hardened. I can tell he probably uses a brand of soap I would hate the smell of. He looks as though he doesn't need to shave every day. My husband had a beard. But, I remind myself, that doesn't matter now. What I prefer is no longer of concern.

∘ ∘ ∘

We are allowed outside for an hour each day, into a fenced pen off the north wing. It is full of plastic lawn chairs, and the women who have been here awhile push to get chairs in the sun. They undress down to their underwear and work on their tans. Other women beeline to an aerobics class in the far corner. The fences are topped with barbed wire. Guards sit in booths and observe. So far I've just walked inside the perimeter and looked through the chain link. The land beyond is razed save for the occasional stubborn stump. Weeds and thorny bushes grow everywhere. This is a newer facility. Decades from now, perhaps young trees will shade it, which, I think, would make it cozier. Far off, the forest is visible; a shaky line of green from the swaying trees. Though coyotes prowl the barren tract, it is the forest that, to me, seems most menacing. It is so unknown.

On my walks I often must step around a huddle of women from another floor (the floors mostly keep together, socially); they form a human shield around a woman on her knees. She is digging into the ground with a serving spoon from the cafeteria. It is bent, almost folded, but still she scrapes at the pebbly soil. There are runners who try to escape at night. They think they will fare better on their own. I don't think I could do it. I'm too domestic for that kind of thing.

o o o

Four weeks in, and I have gotten to be friends with the women on my floor. It turns out we're all bakers. Just a hobby. Each night one of us whips up some cookie or cake from memory, or from a recipe found in the old women's magazines lying around the compound, and we sample it, drink tea, chat. It is lovely to be with women. In many ways, this is a humane shelter. We are women with very little to do and no certain future. Aside from the daily work of bettering ourselves, we are mostly left alone. I like the women

7

on my floor. They are down-to-earth, calm, not particularly jealous. I suspect we are lucky. I've heard fights in the night on other floors. Solitary, in the basement, is always full. As is the infirmary. A woman on the fifth floor who had just been chosen was attacked while she slept. Slashed across the cheek with a razor blade. The story goes that when the Placement Team contacted the husband-to-be with the news, he rejected her. There she was, all packed and about to begin a new life. When she returned from the infirmary with tidy stitches to minimize the scarring, she crawled into that same bed where her blood still stained the sheets. If she had been on our floor, I would have changed the sheets for her. And I know the others would have too. That's what I mean about feeling lucky.

Last week, our girl Marybeth was chosen and sent to a farm near Spokane. We made her a care package; we wrote out recipes on index cards for the treats we'd baked together so she could always remember her time here if she chose to. When we handed it to her, she cried. "I'm not ready," she whimpered. "I still miss him." A couple of us encouraged her, "Just do your best." We stood in a circle embracing, and Marybeth did not want to let go. Eventually the guard led her away; we could hear her trying to catch her breath until the elevator doors closed.

o o o

A window has blinked to life across the road. A man is awake, like me. He pads around his small room in pajamas—the same as ours, hospital blue. I want to be seen, so I stand in my window. He sees me, steps to his window, and offers a quiet wave. I wave back. We are opposing floats in a parade.

If we had been poor and I had died, my husband would be over there now, waiting for someone to want him. How strange to worry about being wanted, when we had been wanted by each other so confidently. Most people reach the age of exemption before their partner dies and they are allowed to simply live alone. Who would want them, anyway? Ideally, you marry the man you love and get to stay with him forever, through everything you can think to put each other through, because you chose to go through it together.

But I had not prepared for this. Had he? Had my husband kept some part of himself separate so he could give it to someone else if he needed to? Was it possible I had managed to withhold something of myself without even realizing it? I hoped so.

I look around my small cinder-block room, painted a halfhearted pink, the desk too large for the unread library book on it. I had a picture of us hidden under my mattress. It was one of those pictures couples take when they are alone in a special place, at a moment they want to remember. We smooshed our heads together and my husband held the camera out and snapped the picture. We look distorted, ecstatic. One night, I fell asleep while looking at it; it dropped to the floor, was found at wake-up, and was confiscated. I still can't believe I was so careless.

In bed, I imagine my husband lying beside me, warming the rubber-coated mattress, beneath the thin sheet so many women have slept under before me. My scalp tingles as I think of him scratching it. We rub feet. Then I have to picture him dissolving into the air like in a science-fiction movie, vaporized to another planet, grainy, muted, then gone. The sheet holds his shape for a moment before deflating to the bed. I practice not feeling a thing.

o o o

A few women on other floors have been chosen and will leave tomorrow. I can smell snow in the air pushing through the crack where the window insulation has peeled away. The late fall has given way to winter. When it is too cold, we aren't let outside for activities in the pen. I would give anything to run through a field and not stop. I have never been the running-through-fields type.

Being chosen seems bittersweet. I imagine many of us wouldn't mind living out our days at the shelter in the company of women like ourselves. But then again, it wouldn't always be us. The woman who moved into Marybeth's old room liked to start fights. She told me my muffins were dry. She squeezed one in my face; it crumbled between her fingers. She crept into sweet Laura's room and cut a chunk of her long, shiny hair with safety scissors. Laura was forced into a bob that didn't suit her. Luckily, this woman was very beautiful and was chosen after only four days. We're waiting for her replacement. Even though there is uncertainty in being chosen, it seems more uncertain to remain among the women, a sentiment I've seen expressed in the manual.

o o o

Something very special has happened. I met my window friend. He came over with the others from the men's shelter for bingo. This happens occasionally. It keeps everyone socially agile.

Even though we wave across a wide road, when he walked in I recognized him instantly—the darkness of his hair and the general line of his brow. The nights we wave have become important to me. It's nice to be seen by a man.

My window friend spotted me, too, stopped in the doorway and waved. I waved back, and we laughed. A tiny, forgotten thrill bubbled up in me.

He sat next to me. Close up I found him handsome. He clowned around, pushed the bingo chips off my board whenever I wasn't looking. He was nervous.

He said, "I'm going to tell you ten bad jokes in a row," and he did, counting on his fingers as he went along, not pausing for my laughter, which made me laugh harder. A guard watched us disapprovingly. We were having too much fun. I guess it goes without saying that relations between shelter dwellers are prohibited. I mean, how could we survive together in the world if we have both ended up in a place like this?

At the end of the evening a whistle blew and the men began to shuffle out. Again my window friend stood in front of me and waved and I did the same. But this time he touched his open hand to mine. I felt us quake like animals that have been discovered where they shouldn't be and have no time to run, no place to run to.

The next night, after we waved, I undressed in the window, the lights bright behind me. He placed his hands against the glass as if to get closer and watched.

Tonight, his light isn't on and so we don't wave, but still,

I undress in front of my lit window. I can't know if he's watching from the darkness, or who else is watching, for that matter. I loved my husband. I mourn his tenderness. I have to believe that someone out there is feeling a kind of tenderness for me. I'll take it any way I can.

○ ○ ○

I've been moved to another floor. Someone from the men's shelter reported me, and my Case Manager thought it best that I occupy a room in the back of the building. Now I overlook the pen.

For days, I feign illness and stay in bed. I hear the groups of women doing their outside activities. It is a cyclical drone of laughing, arguing, calisthenic counting, and loaded silence.

When I do go outside to the pen, the women from my old floor give me hugs and we try to talk like the old days, but it's different. A couple of friends have been chosen and are gone, and now there are some new women. Even one to replace me; she lives in my room and has a view across the road to the men's shelter and my window friend. Her name is even close to mine. She told me that the women sometimes slip and call her by my name. She told me this to comfort me, with a sympathetic pat on my arm. But it doesn't help. Is there any difference between us beyond a few letters in our names?

They pass me some of the cookies and sweets they bake, though they are always a few days old and crumbly, stale; nothing like the warm, fresh treats I was so fond of. I've started throwing them away, but I won't tell them that, because I like that they still think of me.

The women on my new floor are mostly concerned with escape. They are dogged. Their desire scares me. But there are two nice women. They don't try to run, or not that I've heard about. Our way out of here is to get chosen. So we swap tips from the different pamphlets we've read. We don't bake.

o o o

The alarm sounds.

It sounds when someone runs.

Floodlights sweep over the field, then through my window. I hear the yowling of dogs as they smell their way through the night, tracking some woman. Curiously, I find myself rooting for her. Perhaps I'm half asleep but, peering out my window, I think I can see her. As the lights search the wasteland between the pen and the forest, a shadow moves swiftly, with what seems like hair whipping behind, barely able to keep up with the body it belongs to.

There's nowhere to hide before the forest line. The runner needs a good head start. I doubt she got it. They never seem to. And yet they always try. What are they looking for? Out there, it's cold and dark. No guarantee of food or money or comfort or love. And even if you have someone waiting for you, still it seems such a slippery thing to depend on. Say my window friend and I ran. Would he love me outside of here? Could I ever be sure? I barely know him.

I picture myself running. My nightgown billowing behind me, my hair loosening from a braid as I speed along. Finally it comes undone and free. I hear the dogs behind me. I see the forest darkness in front of me. From across the field a figure races toward me. But I'm not scared. It's him. My friend. We planned it. We're running so that when we reach the woods we can be together. I feel hopeful to be running across this field toward something I want, and I don't remember the last time I felt such a thing. Just like that, I know why the women run.

I find at the end of this fantasy I am weeping, and so I write it down in a letter to my friend. I write it as a proposition, though I'm not sure it is one. I just want to know if he would agree to it. It's another way of asking, if we weren't both poor wretches, would he choose me? I don't know why, but it's important. I'm desperate to find out. Maybe I've changed. The manual says that in order to move on, we must change. But this change feels more like a collapse. And that is not how the manual says it will feel.

I open my window and the wind pinks my cheeks. I like it. The wind brings the smell from the field and even from the trees. It smells good out there, past where I can see. The dogs are silent now. Maybe the runner made it. I shake my head at the night. I know it's not true.

○ ○ ○

My window friend is gone.

At bingo I search for him. I want to explain my absence, tell him I was moved, while discreetly slipping the letter into his pocket. I can't find him. Another man follows me around, trying to grab my hand; he whispers that he has hidden riches no one knows about. Finally a guard from the men's shelter intervenes, takes the man by the arm. I ask about my friend, and it turns out he was chosen. The guard says he left a few days ago. I ask how many exactly. "Just two," he says, a little sheepishly. I'm destroyed. I say, "Two is not a few," and return to my room. It is painted a buzzing shade of yellow, and I hate it. The desk is even bigger and emptier now that I've stopped pretending to read. The floodlights from the pen have been left on. They blaze through my window all night.

The next day I slog to lunch, but I can't eat. I play with my food until the cafeteria empties. Then my Case Manager calls me in. Her eyebrows are raised, imploring. She opens a file, and in it is the letter I wrote to my window friend. I had hidden it under my mattress. I can't even muster surprise. Of course they would find it.

"I wasn't really going to run," I say. "It was just a fantasy."

"I know."

She pushes the letter to me.

I read it. My handwriting is looped and sleepy. The pages are worn. I wrote a lot, and reread it obsessively to make sure it was right. Reading it now makes me blush. In the letter, I am begging. My tone near hysterics. I promise that we'll find a house, unoccupied in the woods, abandoned years ago. That we'll forage for our food, but that eventually we'll find work, even though all the jobs are spoken for. I insist we'll be the lucky ones. We'll have a family, a house with a yard. He'll have a nice car, and I'll have nice things. We'll have friends over to dinner. We'll take a vacation each year even if it's a simple one. We'll never put off something we really want to do, or something we want now, like children. We'll never fight over silly things. I won't hold a grudge, and he'll say what he's feeling instead of shrugging it away. I won't be irresponsible. I won't buy bedding we can't afford. And I'll be more fun. I'll be game. I won't insist he tell me where we're going when all he wants is to surprise me. I'll never cook him things he doesn't like because I think he should like them. I won't forget to do the small things like pick up the dry cleaning or rake the leaves in our yard.

Of course, I'm writing to my husband.

It reads as if we're fighting and he's stormed out, is spending nights on a friend's couch. Here is my love letter, my apology: please come home.

I look up.

"Be sensible," my Case Manager says, not without some kindness. "I can't put your name on any list until you've shown you're moving on."

"But when do I grieve?"

"Now," she says, as though I have asked what day it is.

I think of the man from across the road, my window friend. But I can't even remember what he looks like. I try to picture him in his room, but all I see is my husband, waiting, in his plaid pajamas and woolly slippers. He shakes a ghostly little wave. I can tell from his shoulders he is sad enough for the both of us.

o o o

For a couple of weeks I allow myself a little moment. I scrape other women's leftovers onto my plate. I eat the treats my old floor still sends, even though I don't like them. I barter for snacks with some rougher women who somehow had it in them to set up a secret supply business. Now my pants don't fit. My Case Manager finally intervenes. She says even though we live in a progressive time, it's probably not a good idea to let myself go. She gives me some handouts and a new exercise to do that is, literally, exercise. "Get that heart rate up," she says, pinching the flesh above my hip.

I know she's right. We are all dealing with our situation differently. At night, some women cry. Other women bully. Others bake. Some live one life while dreaming of another. And some women run.

Each night a new alarm sounds, the dogs, the lights. In the morning I'll see who looks ragged, as if she spent a futile few hours flying across the barren tract to the forest, only to be recaptured. I'll also look to see if anyone is missing. I still secretly hope she, whoever she was, made it, and I feel twinges of curiosity at the thought of such a life. But they're just twinges. Not motivation. I have nothing to run to. What I want, I can't have. My husband is gone. But while I work to let him go, there are other ways to feel happy. I read that in the manual. I'm willing to try them out. My Case Manager says this is healthy.

o o o

Eight months into my stay at the shelter for widows and other unwanteds, I am chosen. My Case Manager is proud of me.

"That's a respectable amount of time," she insists.

I blush at the compliment.

"The knitting helped," she notes, taking quiet credit for suggesting it.

I nod. However it happened, I'm just glad to have a home.

My new husband's name is Charlie and he lives in Tucson and the first thing he bought with the dowry was a new flat-screen TV. But the second thing he bought was a watch for me, with a thin silver cuff and a small diamond in place of the twelve.

My Placement Team takes me to a diner on the outskirts of town, where Charlie waits in front of a plate of pancakes. He has girlish hands but otherwise he is fine. The Team introduces us and, after some papers are signed, leaves. Charlie greets me with a light hug. He is wearing my husband's cologne. I'm sure it is a coincidence.

I am his second wife. His first wife is in a shelter on a road that leads to the interstate outside Tucson. He tells me not to worry. He didn't cause their broken marriage. She did. I nod, and wish I had a piece of paper so I could take notes.

He asks me how I feel about kids, something he certainly has already read in my file. I answer that I've always wanted them. "We'd been planning," I say. There is an awkward silence. I have broken a rule already. I apologize. He's embarrassed but says it's fine. He adds, "It's natural, right?" and smiles. He seems concerned that I not think badly of him, and I appreciate that. I clear my throat and say, "I'd like kids." He looks glad to hear it. He calls the waitress over and says, "Get my new wife anything she wants." There's something in his eagerness I think I can find charming.

I am not ready for this. But I've been told that someday I'll barely remember that I ever knew my first husband. I'll picture him standing a long way down a crowded beach. Everyone will look happy to be on the beach. Something about him will catch my eye, but it won't be his wave, or his smile, or the particular curl of his hair. It will be something I wouldn't associate with him. It will be the pattern on his bathing shorts; bright stripes, red floral or maybe plaid. I'll think something like, "What a nice color for bathing shorts. How bright they look against the beige sand." And then I'll turn my attention to the crashing waves or to some children building a sand castle, and I'll never think of him again. I'm not looking forward to this day. But I won't turn my back on it. As the manual often states, this is my future. And it's the only one I get.

THE WAY THE
END OF DAYS
SHOULD BE

A dead man twists around one of my Doric columns. I chose these columns for their plainness, their strength. I liked imagining people looking up at my home, its smoky leaded windows reflecting their city back at them, the classic Greek proportions held up by simple, democratic design. Tasteful. No frills. I loathe Ionic columns. I don't even acknowledge Corinthians.

The dead man's arm trembles oddly in the water, out of rhythm with the rest of his body. It's most likely dislocated. Perhaps more than dislocated, but I won't investigate. A brown gull does a number on his eye socket.

The man doesn't look familiar, so I don't believe him to be one I've already turned away.

When the world first flooded, the men who came to my door asking for handouts respectfully left when I said no. They'd survived once before and would do it again. There were other options still. Colonies remained above water with homes to take refuge in. They speckled the rising sea.

Now those colonies are underwater, most of the inhabitants drowned. Any survivors are desperate.

The other day a man in what looked to have once been a pretty fine suit knocked on my door. The suit was now in ruins, the arms shredded like party streamers from his shoulders. Sea salt ghosted his face. Some sand, or maybe a barnacle, clung to his neck. A blue crab scuttled under his hand-stitched lapel. But I mostly noticed his loosened tie because it was definitely designer—it was a kind of damask pattern, but nontraditional. Of course, only designers change designs. It's why we used to pay so much for them. We paid for innovation.

This man in the nice suit asked for food and water, then tried to strangle me, choked back tears, apologized, asked to be let in, and when I refused, tried to strangle me again. When I managed to close the door on him, he sat on my veranda and cried.

I've gotten used to these interruptions, of course. Though the strangling is new.

I don't blame them. If I'd been one of the unprepared, I'd be desperate too. They come to my door, see that I am clean, are dazzled by the generator-fed lights. They sense I have rooms full of provisions, that my maid's quarters are filled with bottled water, cords of wood in the exercise annex, and gas in the garage. They ogle my well-fed gut. I am dry. They are embarrassed, filthy, smell of fish. They get back on their driftwood, or whatever they use to keep their heads above water, and paddle next door to my neighbor's. If I were them, I would overtake someone standing dry in the doorway of a fine home. I wouldn't give up so easily. But these men are not me. For starters, they're awfully weak due to not eating. But still. I don't like the change. I miss the old days when, though they happened to be begging, they were still gentlemen who understood that hard work was their ticket to success. I'll need to carry a knife to the door next time.

o o o

It was happening just like they said it would. Things never happen like they say they will. That I was living to see it felt kind of special, truth be told. Like a headline. HISTORY IN THE MAKING!

My neighbor's house still stands, and across a new tiny sea roiling from trapped fish and unprepared people, one additional cluster of houses remains, perhaps four in all. Day and night, people hang out the windows waving flags of white bedsheets and shouting. What kind of message is that? Surrender? To whom? I'll bet they have no food and water. My neighbor's house shakes from the extra people crammed inside. Each of the ten bedrooms probably holds a small village of newly homeless vagrants he's rescued. I told him to prepare. "I know this sounds crazy," I said. We haven't always gotten along, but I thought it the neighborly thing to do. You'd think he'd be grateful. But instead he just crowds our last parcel of heavenly land with bums. If I open the windows I will smell the house, its burdened toilets and piss-soaked corners. The shallow but rising sea moat between our homes is rank with sewage. The tide takes it away, but more always comes.

In the old days, I would have left a letter in his mailbox about this or that neighborly issue. One time, the mail carrier warned me that it was illegal for non–mail carriers to put things into mailboxes. "It's just a note," I reasoned when she tried to give it back to me. "See how overgrown his hedges are?" She stared unbudgeably hard, held the letter steady between us. "Why can't you just leave it there for him?" I snarled. I slammed the door in her face, and the next morning I found it stuffed in with my own mail, in my own mailbox. On it she had scrawled petulantly, *Only I can put this in the mailbox and I won't do it!*

Through my great-room window, I can see that his grand staircase, with its audacious pineapple-carved finials, is littered with men, women, and children. The way they lie about, it looks as though there's one whole family to a stair. A boy dangles from a dusty crystal chandelier. I watch an old woman topple over a railing while maneuvering through the immense spiral shantytown. What a shame. But you can't let everyone in. There would be no end to it.

I run a finger over the great-room mantel. Dead skin, infiltrated ash. Too bad the housekeeper has most likely perished.

○ ○ ○

Someone knocks on my door—insistent and angry rather than timid and begging. I grab that kitchen knife.

On my veranda stands a man holding himself up by the door knocker, his wiry muscles about to tense themselves off his bones. His face is unshaven, neglected. He has the skinny corpse and fat face of a drunk, and when I pull the door open he attempts to keep hold of the knocker and falls in, face-plants on my entryway Oriental.

"Whiskey," he moans, reaching for some imaginary tumbler.

I think about swiping his open palm with my blade, but there is something about him that I like. His request is original. At least he's trying.

Where my driveway used to curve into a grand circular turnaround, the waves are mincing: they hiss, churn up crud and fish parts. But the ones in the distance are large and smooth; they conceal the city I used to look out at. They roll long like bedsheets drying in the wind, and I can feel their break.

I didn't think I could tire of the sound of crashing waves, but it never ends. It holds your attention like someone who can't stop coughing. It grates. It might be nice to listen to something else for a change. Plus, I'm tired of my music.

I know I probably shouldn't, but I kick his feet toward an ornamental umbrella stand, get him full-bodied into the house, and close and lock the door. He wants whiskey? I don't care for it, and I have too much as it is. Besides, I've always liked having drinkers around. They often surprise.

∘ ∘ ∘

The man—he grumbles that his name is Gary—doesn't even take the stack of crackers I offer him. He flings them like dice and messily pours another glass.

"Ice," he slurs.

I shake my head. The fridge is dormant. My food is canned. And the kind of whiskey I keep should be enjoyed sans ice.

He's so at ease in his stupor. Though he arrived sopping,

if he asked me what's with all this water, I wouldn't be the least surprised.

Now he wears one of my bespoke suits, bespoken on a trip abroad, in fact. He wears it like he's a metal hanger, but it's a bit tight on me. I'm not ashamed. I live a good life.

I make a list of chores for him, written out like a contract.

"If you're going to live here, you're going to work," I say, and slide it over for him to sign. He does so without reading. Irresponsible.

So I read it to him. "The contract states that in exchange for room and board, Gary will guard the house and take care of any beggars or intruders. He will refill the flush buckets with seawater so we can flush our toilets like civilized people. He will throw our empty cans, bottles, and uneaten food out the back door each night to avoid smells. He will help the owner with weekly cleanings of the house. He will perform all other duties the owner asks."

There are plenty of extra bedrooms for him to stay in, but it's my house. So for the first night, I set him up on the study love seat with some fine sheets and a goose down pillow. He scrunches into it, keeping one eye open as he sleeps, one foot up on the coffee table and the other leg bent, perfectly right-angled, foot flat on the floor, ready. For what? To run? Though the water is creeping closer to the house, I'm not sure that's it.

∘ ∘ ∘

The far stand of houses is gone. Where there should be rickety multifamilies, I see water flat like a prairie, occasional whale spouts blurring the horizon line. The glare off all that water is like looking right at the sun.

I see my neighbor padding around the sleeping bodies in his halfway home for derelicts. He is dressed in a tattered robe, his beard long and unkempt. I can practically smell him.

I catch his eye across the moat and mime a drowned body, limbs, head, and tongue hung and bobbing, and then point to where the houses had stood. He looks, rubs his eyes, and drops to his knees. Some of the criminals he's invited into his home take this opportunity to rob him. Their hands work him over, dig in his bathrobe pockets, his hair, while he shudders with grief. Something is yanked from under his arm, and they disperse so quickly it's like they were never there. I shiver. My neighbor is taller than I am, and stronger. What would become of me if I had hundreds of people crammed into my house? I'd have no food left. I'd be bullied out of my master suite. I might even lose my life. I am once again grateful for Gary. He wants nothing from me except my whiskey, and has the build of a welterweight or a thief: small and wiry, someone who can put you in a headlock before you feel his touch.

As my neighbor wipes his tears, I shrug in commiseration. But he just shakes his head at me with disappointment, like I'm the one who just robbed him; I'm the water that tore those houses down.

And here I thought I was being neighborly.

∘ ∘ ∘

Unless he's sneaking into the pantry late at night, I doubt Gary has eaten a morsel since his arrival. I notice no dent in my supplies, except the whiskey, which is already half gone. I've always known liquor to be the stuff of preservation, so I'm only a little surprised. The other night, I crumbled some crackers into a half-full bottle to see if he would take to the sustenance, and he roared, smashed the bottle against the marble table where we dine. The noise was exhilarating. Normally the only sound is the constant murmur of the sea around us. Some nights I hear displaced loons call out to find their mates, or human calls from the boats of survivors looking for land, shelter. Their voices travel low across the water and get trapped within the walls of my bedroom. Sometimes I hear music from my neighbor's house. Not often. Usually it's dreary, but on occasion a piano is tuned, accompanied by some squeaky string instrument. People stomp feet and call out. It's rustic. One night I heard a wavering wedding march and imagined a bride, in a dress of pinned white towels, making her way through the mob to stand with her groom. Two people desperate to have what they think is love before the big end—it was hard not to feel something.

Gary doesn't always hear noise, or even conversation. He sleeps undisturbed at strange intervals, like a pet. It's pleasant enough. When I need him, he is a great bodyguard. When a knock echoes through the house, I send him to the door with instructions to gut-punch the supplicant men. And he does it. They fall backward from shock and he slams the door. Once a woman came to the door, bent like a hook, and Gary paused and then turned to me miserably. I shrugged. Most bands of vagrants send the men out of respect, but clearly they were desperate. They hoped we might treat a woman differently. I saw two tense shapes in a rowboat just beyond the south wing of the house. What could Gary do? Some people hang on to old ideals. I do not. But I couldn't make a man like Gary do something he didn't feel good about. He has integrity. I pointed to my knee. He gave hers a halfhearted kick and she crumbled. He shut the door gently. I hope he feels like this is his home too.

o o o

Gary has allowed me to shave him. He sits on the edge of my tub and snoozes while I hot-towel him, lather his face and neck. I wag the razor clean in a silver bowl of Evian. He looks more and more like a business partner; his graying temples lend him an executive air. He wears my suits—navy, charcoal, funeral black—and sometimes I put him in a tie. The ties are specks of color on his landscape. The world outside is all dark water, cloud, and night, dotted with faded plastic garbage, the clothing of the dead, the red brick of my neighbor's house. A bit of color brings out Gary's eyes.

I leave him to clean up, and a while later he tumbles through the bathroom door and knocks into the armoire. He is dangerously intoxicated and half dressed.

He crouches before me in my reading chair, sticks a soiled finger into my mouth, claws my lower jaw open. He strokes the caverns of my back teeth. I taste sour salt.

"Where's *your* gold?" he asks, like a child who thinks everything is his mirror.

I lean back from his brackish finger. "I have porcelain fillings."

He is blank.

"You can't see them. They blend in with my teeth. They're better."

His face threatens a smile, which would be a first, but instead his mouth gapes wide; it's like a California riverbed, shallow gold in every hole.

He taps one. "My bank," he says, and howls irresistibly. I'm transported to another time when men brawled and kept their money in a sock. I slouch luxuriously into my Queen Anne. Gary gulps from the bottle and falls into my bed. He's wearing a pair of my paisley silk boxers, his legs knobby and bowed like a baby bird's, and a woven dress shirt, the French cuffs gutted. I'm sure he has no idea how to fasten them with cufflinks, or why he would.

"Gary."

He murmurs from just below sleep.

"Did you ever think you'd be sleeping under down, in a well-appointed room, clean-shaven, in French tailored shirts and silk underwear?"

He strains an eye open, seems to ponder it, like maybe he can see where I'm going with all this.

"I'm just saying, I think we have a pretty good thing here. We are at the height of land. We have a very handsome house. It doesn't smell, doesn't leak, isn't crowded. Think of the wind. It sweeps over the entire sea, gathers all that fresh air just to deposit it at our doorstep. We have loads of food. More than we could ever eat, really. We drink imported water."

I suck at a bottle to demonstrate.

"The whiskey won't last, but I'm sure we can think of something. There's other liquor. I have port. Several vintages. All told, Gary, we have a pretty nice life."

He yawns. Perhaps he'll take this moment to drain an-other bottle. He gazes toward my neighbor's house.

I'm wondering if he's heard me when he mumbles, "We're homeless."

I don't know what he means. "Don't be absurd," I say. I'm certainly not homeless. And neither, now, is he.

But then I think maybe I do understand his meaning, looking at the lapping endless sea, which for once stretches beyond metaphor and actually is endless.

Homeless is a term of destitution. We're not hanging out of windows, waving blankets; we're not trod upon by soggy feet like my neighbor. But undeniably we are experiencing a lack. I respond, "Friend, we are *worldless*." I let my new word linger.

Gary sniffles and paws at his face, and then I see a glistening on his cheek.

"Gary, are you *crying*?" I mock tenderly.

He scowls and pulls the blanket right up under his nose, clutches the whiskey close to his heart, and pretends to sleep.

o o o

I hear murmuring outside the house.

A boat creaks offshore. A sail of ragged cloth, multicolored swatches crudely stitched together, barely registers the wind. I can make out the figures of two men swim-walking their way to our door while others wait in the boat. They gaze admiringly at the house. As they should.

"Gary," I hiss.

A minute later he shuffles into the entryway, bringing with him a scent of something savory. Not whiskey, I notice, and think it odd.

"Men are coming. See what they want."

Gary peeks out from behind the drapes, allows his eyes to adjust, and nods. I hand him a knife and he slips out the front door to meet the men.

He returns with a note in a bottle.

"They're from next door," he says, slurring slightly.

"They have a boat next door?" Should we have a boat? I hadn't thought about surviving outside my home. Would I even want to? It seems so awful out there. But maybe it's something I should get Gary on, just in case. Boatbuilding. How turn-of-the-century.

The note is scrawled on the back of a soup label:

> *Dear Neighbor, might you have some food and water to spare? My men will ferry it over. We are running dangerously low. Might you have some room to spare? I'll send clean women and children. We're greatly overcrowded. The walls seem to be buckling. I am concerned. Respectfully.*

I crumple the letter. The nerve. "No way."

Gary looks surprised, which surprises me.

"But we have spare food."

"What do you know about food?" I yell.

"You said we had more than enough."

"I did not!"

"You did." He sulks.

"That was before. We're running very low. You eat too much."

"We have a lot of food," he mumbles again.

"I suppose you know best. I suppose you're the decision maker now. I guess you'll be telling me we should invite them over."

"Would it be so terrible to let some in?"

"Yes!"

Gary looks up at the grand staircase, considers each wing. "There's room."

I throw my hands up. "You're unbelievable! He's scamming you!" I'm ashamed of the squeal in my voice, but I can't control it. "His house was always a wreck. Cracked windows. Bricks crumbling. His vines on *my* side of the fence. His portico has *always* looked like that. His house is *buckling*? Well, his upkeep is for shit."

Gary gazes longingly at the upstairs hallways, as if fantasizing that they are crowded with laughing children and pretty women.

"They'll ruin everything. Our life. They'll eat more than their share. They'll waste water. They'll drink your whiskey, you know they will."

Gary blushes and looks down at a smudge on the golden maple floors, licks a finger and squats to rub it out. "I don't care," he mutters into the smudge.

"I'll make it simple for you, simple guy. If you want to be with them, then leave." Even as the words come out, I want to take them back. The rest of this life feels impossible without Gary. But I shouldn't have to give up a life I enjoy to harbor the foolish masses. What's the point of living if you can't have the life you want?

Gary turns his gaze to me, and I don't like the look. It's

like we don't even know each other. He slips the knife from his pocket and strides out the door.

They are having words. I can't tell if Gary's is one of the voices. Maybe the men are begging to be let in, and Gary is merely listening, hearing them out. That would be so like Gary.

But maybe the men are begging to be let in and Gary is saying yes. That would be a different Gary, I think.

Then I hear yelling and the grunts of a struggle. The sound escapes across the sea; there is nothing to stop it. I hide in the closet. A lone trench coat hangs there. I wrap myself in it.

A cry of pain leads to the sound of men splashing in retreat.

The front door is opened, then gently clicked shut, as though I am a child and Gary is taking care not to wake me. Feet shuffle away. I crack the door and see the knife lying in the center of the rug. It is smeared with blood and sea scum. I would like to dress his wounds if he has any, but I don't move.

From the study comes the clinking of bottle to glass. A glass this time. What civility. I'm ashamed for doubting him. He knows what is at stake. He is a loyal friend. All is well.

o o o

The new ocean is changing the weather in awful ways, and it's been cold for days. The sky dumps fluffy fist-sized snow-flakes, and then in a blink we are pelted with hail the size of clams. Clumps of sea ice are forming in eddies. The chimney clogs with ice and snow, and smoke billows in from the fire-place. We cough. Gary opens a window. In comes the smell of the fecal moat. We gag. He closes the window.

It occurs to me that if it weren't for the neighbor's over-run house, we might be a little freer in our own. Wouldn't it be nice to stand in the doorway and enjoy the cold breeze and the view? I never used to have much of a view, just all the rooftops below me. But now I have an ocean view.

I'm angry with my neighbor for opening his doors while I closed mine. We should have more control over the end of days. It should be more pleasant somehow. It's the end of days, after all.

I sleep under the pall of my resentment, but then I become vaguely aware of Gary's hand stroking my hair, his sour breath whispering in my ear, *Colleen*. A lesser man might feel threatened by a drunk fondling him in his bed. But I am not a lesser man. I think it's soothing. Another's need is a funny thing. It's so often cloying. But sometimes, with the right person, it can be the most comforting thing in a day. I find that despite everything, in this moment I feel quietly happy.

o o o

A terrible crash wakes me. I reach across the bed, but Gary is not there.

I see nothing through the window, but hear the sea lash-ing at the side of the house, frantic and high. The clouds are thick like insulation and hide any evidence of a moon. Is it large and full and pulling the tides higher, or is this some kind of grand, irreversible shift in things?

I sink into the cold middle of the bed. Then comes another crash, and yelling, and the unforgettable cracking of heavy beams of wood, of walls collapsing. Screams, splashes, cries for help. If I had to guess, I'd say my neighbor's house has just fallen to pieces. I don't want to look, in case I'm right. The surrounding sea would clog with the lifeless, facedown, a simple burial for those who had survived longest. A passing thought: Must I shoulder some blame for this tragedy? I'd believed our stories were separate. I'd begun to think of this earth as my own private sanctuary. Shared with Gary. We could climb higher and higher as the water rose and live out our days in that quaint, functionless widow's walk, until it too was swallowed. I'd always thought it such a romantic scenario. But with our neighbors washed away, I'm suddenly curious what other story we all might have told together. We're each of us survivors, after all. What a pathetic end. How desperate. I fall asleep in a surprising state of grief.

○ ○ ○

In the light of day, my neighbor's house is still standing. The top of the building has caved in on itself. Some bodies float in the surrounding waters, but not many. The bobbing corpses lack the gravitas I imagined. I leave bed to fix myself a plate of crackers and peanut butter.

As I approach the landing, I hear hushed voices and I see my neighbor in the entryway with Gary. They lean in to one another, whispering. It all looks quite friendly, which is surprising.

"Howdy, neighbor." I try for blitheness.

They look up, caught. I scan Gary's face for clues, then my neighbor's.

My neighbor has tried to clean himself up a bit. His clothes look pressed in spots, like he has laid them between stacks of books to mimic the effect of steamers. But they are pieces from different suits, clashing directions of stripes on the jacket and pants, and a checkerboard shirt. His beard is roughly trimmed; big chunks of hair are shorter than other chunks, like he cut it with children's scissors. He looks to be wearing some kind of makeup, a powder or rouge for color.

My neighbor nods in greeting. "We had an accident," he wheezes haltingly. "The roof. Fell in. Top floor. Many dead."

"I know, we heard," I say, mustering horror. Gary looks distraught. Then I say, "We heard it fall, I mean," so my neighbor doesn't think we'd heard from someone else, as though it was gossip.

"I saw the bodies in the moat," I say.

My neighbor looks ashamed and sputters, "We had to. The disease. All the others."

I notice that Gary's suit is rough and wrinkled. I reach out, fondle the fabric. It's damp.

"Gary, have you been *swimming*?"

My neighbor coughs. "Neighbor," he says, beginning a plea.

"What do you want?" I ask, trying to sound friendly, but I can tell by their faces that my tone is pure stone.

"We have to hold up the ceiling."

Gary clears his throat. "There are big posts in the basement."

I snort. "There are not." I'm looking right into his eyes,

and they are mossy green and clean like he is fully awake. We are so close; his breath in my face smells sweet, like warm milk. Then I remember: there are posts in the basement, from the renovation on my Doric columns. Why does Gary know my house better than I?

I glare at him, preparing to accuse them of something, but then my neighbor begins to cry. Gary clamps a hand on my neighbor's shoulder to comfort him. I'm alarmed. Those are my hands.

Sea-foam curls around my neighbor's galoshes, and I suddenly feel woozy. I step back, hug my cardigan close, and realize I've become pointy, emaciated. I'm swimming in this sweater; the cuffs hang off me like I'm wearing my father's clothes. Is this even mine? Haven't I been taking care of myself? I look at Gary. He's lean. But I don't think he's leaner than usual. What is going on here?

"He's going to take the posts," Gary says, making it sound utterly ordinary to give something away. He tightens his grip and guides my shell-of-a-neighbor inside. "Watch the rug," he says, and instinctively I'm grateful. He's thought of me. Of us. Of our things. I try to offer him my most thankful smile, but he is already leading my neighbor through the basement door. "I'll help him," he calls back over his shoulder.

Of course my neighbor will need help. The posts are big and long and were almost too much for the builders to get down there in the first place. And my neighbor is clearly starving. But again, I'm surprised by Gary. When they come out of the basement, I notice that Gary's feet aren't stumbling. He appears strong, almost. He is speaking in full sentences, not slurs. He's concerned and not angry. He directs my neighbor, who is bent and shaky, barely able to hold the post up, toward the door. Gary stands tall, the post balanced easily on his shoulder, like he doesn't feel the weight. I want to check my food supply, but I know that would be wrong. It's his house too.

I watch them float the posts over and disappear into my neighbor's house. I bolt the door. When they come back, let them knock. But then I think, no, it's Gary. I draw the bolt back.

o o o

I stoke the fire all night and wait for the splashing sound of Gary crossing the moat and returning home. I deserve an explanation. I can't sleep without him.

In my neighbor's house, lit by candlelight, I see a crowd gathered around Gary. He appears to be giving a speech. His head is bowed and his hands cover his chest like they are protecting a wound. He is not throwing bottles and sulking. And when he begins to weep, the masses gently reach to comfort him; they place hands on him. My neighbor steps through, the people breaking apart for him, and he and Gary embrace. Gary sobs into his neck.

I crawl to the liquor cabinet. One bottle of whiskey remains. I cough down half and then hurl the bottle at the great window.

I check my food supplies. They don't appear diminished beyond reason, but I suppose there is more food gone than there should be. Didn't there used to be one more pallet by the bed? But that's easily explained by Gary starting to eat.

Had he? I couldn't remember him ever sharing a meal with me, though he always kept me company while I dined. I could live off this food for a while longer, definitely till the end, which feels closer than ever before. But that's not the point, I think as I urinate into the fireplace. Dense smoke erupts and smothers me. I double over, breathless. I wrench the window wide and gasp in that putrid moat. Dawn is breaking. A bloated and sun-bleached cow drifts by, its hide rippling with bugs, its tail end chewed off by some animal, its methaned stomach still intact and about to burst. That will be me. Pale, bloated, and raped in some feeding frenzy by what still lives.

Why did he leave?

Who said he could leave?

o o o

The water in the moat has an eerie heft, like it is about to become slush. I find firm ground near the corner of my neighbor's house, and soon I emerge. Water sloshes out from under my clothes and from my pockets; salt and sand grit my mouth.

I hear the noise of much life inside, hundreds and hundreds of people, but as I pass in front of a window, the commotion stops. When I knock on the front door, it's like the whole world holds its breath. I press my ear to it. Nothing.

"I know you're in there," I yell. "I can see you all from my house."

I hear a cough from inside, and a quick rush to stifle it.

"You stole my food."

Silence.

I pull a note card from my pocket, kept dry in a plastic

baggie. It's an eloquent reminder for Gary of our comfortable life at home, of how I saved him, of our friendship, and of the contract he signed. I find a crack at the top of the door and try to push the note through. Something stops it midslide and pushes it back out.

Gary.

I know it's him on the other side. I palm the door and press my cheek against it. It is slimy with algae. I feel painted onto it.

"Gary!" I yell. "Let me in! I'm cold and wet."

The moon is full. The tide will be high. The water is waiting for orders. I think it wants this house as much as I do.

I could still make it home. I might still touch the bottom of the moat if I head there now. But for what? People begin moving around again inside my neighbor's house. I hear the march of many feet up and down the staircase. A piano is tuned. They are carrying on. I notice for the first time that my neighbor's house sits slightly lower on the hill than mine. We truly were at the height of land. It was not my imagination, or merely a boast. I'm awash with sadness.

"Gary. We had it all."

I sit down on the stoop, and the water rises to my knees. Small fish circle my legs like they are playing a game.

Hawks soar high in the pinking sky. I don't know much about birds, but I imagine they need land somewhere nearby. If they are gulls, they can float on the water. I don't think hawks can do that. Or buzzards circling a kill. If they were albatross, they could fly the length of one giant ocean and never get tired. I've heard they keep ships company on an entire journey and then keep going. There is something in the name that makes me believe this. Albatross. It feels never-ending.

I hadn't considered that somewhere beyond my sight the world might be continuing as normal. If those are hawks, they'll have to return to their treetops, high above houses full of sleeping families, husbands and wives, children lucky enough to be born. Just beyond the curve of the earth, out of my view, skyscrapers could be creaking slightly in the newly blistering wind. Newscasts could be reporting about us, the ones who perished. But I'm still here.

I'm surprised how easy it was for me to believe I was one of the lucky few left. If people are watching this sunset all over the world, then I'm not so lucky after all, sitting up to my chest in cold ocean water that's cluttered with debris and oily with human waste. What makes me so special? I had a house. I had Gary. It felt like enough for the end of days.

Soon someone will need to open the door. They have flush buckets to fill. Cans, bottles, batteries, to toss. Don't they? I could wait.

I try to imagine it: *me* in *there*. Pressing palms, talking about the lives we'd lived. Being nostalgic, but for what? Eating crumbs together? Of course, if they let me in, I'd be expected to give over my house and supplies. They'd paw my antiques. They'd mess up all the beds' bedding. I'd never again enjoy that morning echo of solitary me padding across the floors of my house.

If I go home, I'll live longer. It is indisputable. I don't know what more I could ask for.

"Okay, Gary. Last chance. I'm leaving," I call out. I wait a beat, listening for the door to creak, for curiosity or need to win out.

Instead, I hear laughter behind my neighbor's door.

o o o

I know that soon they will come. Gary will lead them. It could be any minute now. They'll wade, swim, or selectively drown their way across the moat and savagely break through my great window and splinter open the locked front door. It's a quality door. It won't be easy.

Then the water and weather will get in and eat the house from the inside. They'll be left with nothing yet again. I could warn them, but do I have to think of everything?

I wait in the widow's walk, surrounded by soft down pillows, a tower of blankets. I have with me water, crackers, tinned meat, and my two biggest knives, but I hope it won't come to that. I don't think Gary will let it. True, I feel betrayed. He knows all my secrets, what I'm most afraid of, all the combinations, and where anything of worth is hidden. But I will still be his friend. If he'll have me.

The moon rises, dips, rises, dips. The tide rolls in and out. I wait for the end. Frigid air pries itself inside. Even shrouded in blankets, I'm folded over from shivering. I wait for them. Pieces of my neighbor's house are letting go, dropping into the sea. Some break windows as they fall. Is that a piano I hear tinkling, or glass shattering? Is that the sound of singing or of wood creaking to its breaking point? The whole house leans. The wind keens something awful. The sea is knocking, but his door remains shut.

SOMEBODY'S
BABY

Linda swaddled her newborn Beatrice in the butter-yellow blanket the neighborhood women had knitted, and joined her husband in the car. They drove from the hospital, smiling at the baby and each other. They turned onto their street and smiled at their house, which they'd had restored and painted a color they believed would make all the difference in raising their family. Then their smiles vanished.

The man was already in the yard.

They pulled into the driveway, and the man skulked behind the maple. When he saw that they'd seen him, he stepped out from behind it. He loped across the yard, then back.

Linda hugged Beatrice close, let her husband do the job of slamming the car doors, shouting, staring the man down. She felt helpless, and so she scurried quickly to the house, knowing that her husband's attempts to be menacing would fail.

Inside, she watched the man in the yard watch the house. She knew it wouldn't be long before he got inside. He always did.

And so Linda never left the house unless she had to. She locked up after her husband went to work. She installed bars over the windows. In the nursery she stood behind the curtains while Beatrice slept, and she watched the man. When she took out the garbage, she clutched her baby to her chest and locked eyes with the man as she stumbled past with the leaking bag. But all it would take was a brief moment; she knew that. If she spent too long looking for something in the fridge. If she sliced her finger cutting carrots and grimaced in pain. If she fell asleep while Beatrice napped. It would be some small thing.

Linda had asked her neighbors to call if they ever saw the man approach. She could hear them hold their breath cautiously over the phone.

We'll try, but Linda, you know, they'd start to say, and Linda would hang up. She knew what they wanted to tell her, and she didn't want to hear it. At least if she could see him, if someone could see him, it meant he wasn't already inside.

But then one day a package was delivered. She signed for it carelessly, looking instead at the man in the yard. Inside the house, she drew out a knife to slice the box tape, and noticed the package wasn't addressed to her. It wasn't even for someone on the block. The deliveryman had given her a stranger's package. He was already down the driveway in his truck.

Wait, she called, running to stop him before he pulled away.

He jumped from the truck to meet her, and something about his quickness made her suddenly remember the man in her yard. How easily her mind had let go of that burden.

Some dumb box was all it took. She dropped it, ran into her house screaming. But it was too late. The man had come and gone, and he had taken Beatrice with him.

o o o

There's nothing you can do, her neighbors reminded her as she grieved. A few had stopped by bearing casseroles, homemade jams.

You'll get past this, and then you'll have another, they said.

But he'll just take that one, she cried.

Maybe not, they exclaimed hopefully. Sometimes he only takes one!

I couldn't bear it if he took another, she sobbed.

There, there. They smoothed her hair, squeezed the tension from her hands. We know what you're going through.

Then why are you smiling?

Because we know you'll try again and have the family you want. They beamed at one another. We did.

Linda sniffed. Well, maybe I'm not like you.

What a shame, her neighbors thought. Imagine giving up a family—a *family*—because it was hard. Of course it was hard—the man, the fear, the pummelling grief. But giving up only brought emptiness. She could have such a nice family with just a little more effort.

o o o

But a few years later Linda did have another child, a boy she named Lewis, and she cried with relief as the doctor laid him on her chest to nurse. Linda looked at his face, and it was as if she'd never seen another baby before, he was so perfect. She felt whole. She was glad she'd tried again.

Are you sure you don't want me to drive you home? her husband asked, bending into her car to touch Lewis's warm belly again for no reason. His car idled beside him.

Go to work. Linda smiled. I'm fine. She really felt fine. She believed everything was going to be fine this time.

But when she pulled into her driveway with Lewis, the man was in the yard, waiting.

Linda shook. Tears wet her cheeks, but she didn't even realize she was crying. Lewis fussed against the new bad feeling he sensed.

Please leave, she choked. The man picked at his teeth.

She cradled her son's head and stooped, picked up a rock from the worn area between the asphalt and the grass. She threw it at the man. It landed to his left. She threw another and it hit his shoulder but he didn't move, just rubbed the spot with his other hand.

Don't you have enough children already? she cried, then ran to the house and slammed the door behind her.

She drew all curtains, triple-locked all doors, yanked on the window bars to test their strength. What did it matter, though? He's not going to break in. He's going to walk right in when I make a mistake. It'll be my fault, she thought as she settled Lewis into his crib. He looked up at her with moist eyes and shook his limbs in a baby fit. His mouth opened and closed whether he wanted it to or not; his tongue seemed at times too big for his wet mouth. She'd forgotten about all the things babies do, and how pleasing it is to watch them. She watched Lewis for days and nights. She didn't sleep. She didn't want to take any chances.

During one of his late-afternoon naps, she rocked in the rocking chair and watched Lewis moving in his sleep. It looked as if he was wrapping imaginary yarn around an imaginary spindle, making an imaginary bundle he would then stick into his mouth. She got lost in the involuntary turning of his arms. She imagined the two of them flying a kite, her tiny baby in a crib in the middle of a hay-yellow meadow, unraveling a spindle of string into the air as she helped it along, the kite lifting higher with each rotation. But a knot formed and she had to crawl up the string to untangle it. Just as the knot came free, she heard an iron gate creak and saw the man coming across the meadow for Lewis. She shimmied down the string and every inch she slid the man got an inch closer so that in an agonizing way they would each reach Lewis at the same time, and then what? She slid faster and the man walked faster. Then Lewis, with a laugh, let out more string on the spindle, and Linda rose higher, yelling for him to stop, but by then she was too high. The man kept inching forward, and she knew, because of her own foolishness, she was going to lose this baby too. Then she was above the clouds and could no longer see. But she felt the slack as Lewis was taken, imagined him dropping the string in fright as she was set adrift into the sky.

She woke slumped in the rocking chair, disoriented by the dimness of early evening. A reverberation, some disturbance, hung in the air. The alarm clock glowed a witchy green through the darkening room. Panicked, she turned on the light. A baby lay there. He looked like Lewis, but perhaps it was some trick and the man had swapped her child with another, a placeholder she could never love. She slipped Lewis out of his clothing and checked his body to be sure. A birthmark behind his left knee. And then, knowing that, when she looked into his cranky eyes she could see it was Lewis.

Throughout the house, she felt the man's absence. He had been there. The front doorknob held on to just the briefest warmth from his grasp. Next time she would not wake up. She knew that. And the man would not leave the yard until he had Lewis.

o o o

Linda turned to the women in the neighborhood. They'd been so encouraging when she'd gotten pregnant again. But now her neighbors were not helpful.

If there were enough of us on the lookout, I'm sure he would leave us alone, Linda pleaded.

What are we supposed to do, patrol in front of your house all day and night?

All of us?

We have our own families to take care of!

They gathered in Helen's living room for their monthly block association meeting; Helen was the president. But none had come expecting a new idea to be discussed. Now they looked rumpled, when a moment before they had been very put together.

But if we shared the burden, took turns, we could protect our children.

You mean, protect *your* child, Helen clarified in a presidential way, looking around for agreement. The women nodded at this highlighted unfairness.

He's *your* responsibility, complained a woman whose name Linda always forgot. She lived in a red house. Linda had heard a rumor: The woman had *given* her first child to the man. She'd been too overwhelmed. Linda found it hard to believe.

But we've all had to go through this. Imagine if we worked together—we might never lose another.

Jill from the cul-de-sac touched Linda's arm pityingly. You're upset. It's understandable. And you're right: we have all been through this. So trust me when I say eventually he'll stop taking them, and then you will have some to keep. This is how it works. I lost one. She pulled a picture from her wallet of her own smiling family: a husband, two boys, a girl. They were all school-age but wore clothes shapelessly. See?

Helen picked up a school portrait of a boy with a scared smile. For what it's worth, he's my oldest. But really he was number three, she said. It's all in how you look at a thing. She stroked the picture with her manicured finger. Her voice faltered. I remember when he was so little.

Linda's closest neighbor, Gail, picked a hair from Linda's blouse tenderly. Everyone who wants a family manages to have that family, she said. It just takes some of us longer.

Linda felt numb. How can you just let them go and be done? She hadn't meant for it to sound accusatory, but it must have, because she saw the women had stiffened.

Helen's smile was tight. Let me demonstrate something. She pointed to the baby in Linda's arms. What's his name?

Linda squeezed, and he squirmed. Lewis.

And your first? The name? Helen demanded.

Linda hesitated. All she could think of was Lewis, his warmth, his breath. The name Lewis hung lonely in her brain, a place where a minute ago many thoughts had raced.

Helen looked around the circle. I believe I've made my point, she said, and the women nodded. They weren't the ones who needed convincing.

She knelt in front of Linda. When they're gone, they're gone. Have another—start trying now—and hope for the best. She pinched Lewis's cheek roughly and sighed. Meeting adjourned.

Everyone looked drained. They'd never dealt with someone like Linda before.

Linda walked down the road. It was only half a block to her home with the family-friendly paint, so many locks, the man in the yard. She kept thinking, Lewis, Lewis, Lewis. Then a small yellow bird swooped by her on its way from one streetlamp perch to another, and she remembered: Beatrice.

o o o

Why don't you ever stay up to watch over Lewis? she asked her husband. She no longer slept. Their relationship was strained.

I support our family by going to work. If I don't sleep, then I don't work, and we don't eat, he replied.

She wiped the counter again. If we don't have a child, we don't have a family.

He laughed. That's not true at all. You'd be here. My job is to support you. If *you* go away, I have no one to support.

But if Lewis goes away, well, then I have you to support, and then we make another one, and then I support the both of you. That's what a family is. He said it as if he thought she was dumb.

And what if that one gets taken? Her voice cracked.

He realized she wasn't just being contrary but was actually upset. He pulled her close. Shh, shh, he consoled. Don't worry, he rarely takes a third. I can count the number of threes on one hand.

She stiffened. A third? You're not even pretending there's hope for Lewis.

He frowned. Be nice. I'm not the enemy here. He wiped a tear from her cheek.

But she too believed the man would take Lewis. And that he'd take their third child. And their fourth. It would happen to her. Something in the way he was there as she pulled in from the hospital. As if he had a nose for her, for her joy. Maybe it was conceited to think she was different somehow, whether because she felt the need to protect Lewis, or because she felt targeted. She didn't know if it was bad to suspect that the world had its sights trained on her in particular, and that the world could go either way—it could spare her or take a shot. She felt shot at every day of her life since she'd begun having children.

o o o

Linda placed an ad for guards. Must be able to walk and be on feet all day, it read, must be able to work nights. She hired two men recently laid off from a manufacturing plant. They were machinists, wore their machinist jumpsuits and so looked official, uniformed in dark blue with patchy grease stains. They worked the night shift. She hired two more men from the neighborhood, downsized from their city office jobs. Their wives disapproved, but the men insisted it was good work. They worked the day shift. Their wives looked away when they had to drive by. They found it vulgar, their husbands pacing Linda's lawn, guarding just one baby, and not even their own.

But Linda had more time to look at Lewis now that she wasn't always looking at the man in the yard. She memorized Lewis's face. She saw tiny red bumps on his cheeks that she hadn't noticed before. They were like the friendliest sandpaper. She watched him preen as he slept, his small hands fluttering over his face like a shy person's would. On mornings, he smelled of decaying leaves. She bonded with him as she'd read she would in parenting books.

o o o

One night, while Linda bathed Lewis in the kitchen sink, his pale skin masked by the bubbles of baby soap, someone tapped on the window. The figure glowed white under a floodlight, and Linda was startled until she saw it was Gail. The woman stood in a juniper bush under the window, black soil crumbling into her clogs.

I wanted to bring you this Bundt cake, but the wonder twins wouldn't let me in, Gail yelled through the closed window. She held up a cake wrapped in foil.

Linda sighed as she unlocked the door. I know. I had hoped it could feel a bit friendlier. They throw rocks. People have complained.

Sour grapes. They're just mad they didn't think of it first. Gail squeezed one of Lewis's soapy wet feet. He splashed his hands in the water. Besides, it's working, isn't it? He's still here.

True. But you snuck past, didn't you?

And of course you'll talk to them about that.

Of course, Linda murmured, and bit her lip. Sometimes it just feels extreme.

You just keep doing what it takes to keep this little one safe. I wouldn't worry about what people are saying.

Linda hadn't considered that people were saying much of anything.

When Gail left, Linda opened the front door and called the guards over. One faced her, while the other remained turned away to watch the man in the yard. The man in the yard strained forward to hear.

Linda whispered, In general, you're doing great.

The men nodded gravely.

But a friend snuck into the backyard tonight.

Impossible, said the guard facing her. We would never let anyone through.

And we patrol the backyard, said the guard with his back to her. Impossible that we wouldn't see your friend.

Not possible, said the guard facing her.

The point is, said Linda, one, I want to be able to see my neighbors. You can let them through. This is a neighborhood. And two, people can't be sneaking around, or you're not doing the job I hired you for. And I have no problem hiring someone else. She said this in a way that was mean on purpose.

The men were quiet for a moment, sniffed the night air to help them process her threat. Streetlights glowed up and down the block. Leaves wrestled their branches. Sprinklers chugged over far-off lawns. They promised it would not happen again.

o o o

It was the men from the block, the neighbor guards, who ultimately let the man inside. One man's child had broken his leg, was in the hospital, and the father skipped his shift to stay by his son's side. The other man from the neighborhood worked alone. The day progressed uneventfully. The guard watched the man in the yard and the man in the yard watched the guard. There was no need to patrol the house in the usual way; the man in the yard wasn't moving. As long as the man never moved, the guards didn't need to either. There's no other danger, the guard thought, as the sun spotlighted the man in the yard. He'd never heard of an accomplice. He was sure he would know if the man had one. Though what if the man decided to bring an accomplice one day, and the guards weren't patrolling? The odds were low. But still. He'd hate to be the one on patrol and not really patrolling on the one day that the man brought an accomplice.

The guard worked this thought over as he turned to urinate into the bushes that lined the house. He watched the man in the window's reflection. The man still hovered behind the maple. The guard glanced down to aim, and briefly closed his eyes in relief. When he looked again, he no longer saw the man behind the maple. He didn't see the man anywhere. For a moment, he thought the man might have moved fully behind the tree to give him privacy. But that was only the briefest wishful thought, because he knew better. He'd been through this. He'd comforted his own hysterical wife twice, and the story was always that she'd looked away for only a second. *Just one second!* And here he had done just that, even though he had promised himself, and Linda, that he wouldn't.

Inside, Linda and Lewis had relaxed into a nap while he nursed. When the guard burst into the room, Linda startled awake to find a cold spot in the crook of her arm.

o o o

Linda felt a warm, damp thing on her cheek. Gail held a compress to her. The ocher of sunset filtered through the blinds. She had slept most of every day since Lewis was taken. She could not leave her bed. She could not rise to lock any doors. Old soiled diapers stewed in the garbage can, and she could not take them to the curb.

Gail pursed her lips. You need to get up, get on with it, she said, a rind of admonishment around the words.

I don't need to do that, Linda replied.

And how do you tell that to your husband?

I don't. Linda made a half attempt to sit up. We don't talk.

Gail shook her head. And how do you intend to make another if you're not talking? She was trying to tease a smile from Linda.

I don't think we will. I think we're done.

She could see that Gail did not understand.

I can't lose another. I'm not sure I'm going to survive losing Lewis.

This feeling will pass. It always does, Gail tried to reassure her.

How long before you felt normal? Linda asked shyly.

How do you mean?

When were you able to move on?

Why don't you rest some more, Gail suggested, and grabbed her purse as if she was about to run.

Wait, Linda said, grabbing a fistful of bedsheet. How many children did *you* lose? She realized she had never asked.

Well, Gail said curtly. None.

How? He didn't come to your yard! she accused.

Well, of course he did. He comes to everyone's yard.

Well, then?

Gail looked uncomfortable. He waited, but then just lost interest. He doesn't want them once they are too old. Then she said, both delicately and proudly, Honestly, I just never made a mistake.

Linda had never heard of a woman not losing any of her children. No one ever talked of such a thing. She had come to believe it was inevitable, like a law of nature, and not a failure on her part. Or she felt like it was a failure on her part—of course it was a *failure*—but because every other woman had the same failure, failure seemed normal, which made her feel normal, which canceled out the feeling of failure.

It's not your fault, Gail said, smoothing out the wrinkles in Linda's sheets, which was her way of saying that it was.

o o o

The women of the block association met in Linda's living room. She distributed coffee in cups, and they passed around a small pitcher of cream and bowl of sugar.

When all their coffee was white and sweet, Helen tapped a spoon against her cup lip. Linda? You called this meeting. So. The women resentfully stopped chatting.

Linda cleared her throat.

I'm going to find the man. I'm going to get my children and any other children who are there.

The women waited for more, like a punch line.

If, she added, the children are still with him.

Finally someone shrieked, To his *house*?

You can't just *go* there.

You can't just *get* them.

The women all talked at once.

It's not done this way, Helen insisted.

What if you go, and, like you said, there are none? And it's just him? said Lorrie, her voice arcing toward panic. I think I would die.

And what if they're all there? asked Nell, who had four children at home, and was one of the few who'd had three taken by the man. What if you get me my children back? She looked around at the women. Am I supposed to want them? Because I don't. I don't want them anymore. As she spoke, she shook her cup carelessly and coffee sloshed onto the carpet.

Nell's right, Gail said. Children grow up so fast. You won't know them anymore. I'm worried you'll be disappointed with what you find.

Linda thought she saw some women blanch when Gail spoke, and was it her imagination, or had several rolled their eyes? She detected a new chill in the air. There was so much she didn't know about these women.

Linda cleared her throat, said shakily, I'll take that risk.

Everyone deflated in her chair. Were the women having the same thoughts she'd had? Could they handle knowing for certain where their children had been? Could they handle having them back? Or were they thinking something else entirely? Perhaps that Linda was a fool.

The women left, one by one. None gave her blessing.

Linda prepared a snack to take with her. She placed it in her purse with her biggest kitchen knife, wrapped in a tea towel so she wouldn't cut herself if she reached for anything.

○ ○ ○

Like in a fable, the man's house was easy to find. It was the kind of place children told each other about at sleepovers, crowded under blankets, their faces lit by flashlights.

Linda followed the man's well-worn trail, which ran like a scar through her neighbors' yards and into the dense, dark woods. The man lived behind them. Had anyone ever ventured this way before? Or had it seemed too dangerous, too unknown? Linda gasped with each breath, not from exertion but from fear of what she would find.

At the end of the trail sat a clearing, and in the clearing sat a house. An original wooden shack situated itself humbly in the center, but a maze of crudely built additions snaked out from all sides and corners, with additions attached to those additions. It stretched out awkwardly, like a foldable ruler. Linda was so close to her own house that she could hear the hammering of a neighbor who was putting in a deck. The trees were the same. If she let her yard go wild, these same types of trees would grow. The maple in his yard was the same size as the maple in hers. On both, leaves had turned poinsettia red.

She entered the house, followed the drone of a television down a zigzag hallway, and entered a living room. Several broken-skinned couches sat facing a small television. The walls were a raw wood, as was the floor under a mosaic of small mismatched rugs flung together to form a larger one.

On the rug was a child's car seat, and in it lay Lewis, asleep. He looked so different from how she remembered him. He was a few months older now, and had already grown too big for the seat. Linda recognized it as hers and was amazed she'd never noticed it was gone. She wondered how many other things the man had taken from her that day besides Lewis.

In an easy chair next to Lewis sat the man, his arm outstretched to rock the car seat. Several children of various ages splayed on the floor, playing a game. They squinted at her, then returned to their game. On the far corner of a sad blue couch, a small girl was curled in a ball, asleep. Her dirty hair was a nest of knots, with some small twigs and mosses tied in.

Linda whimpered.

The man scowled at her. What did you think? he sneered in a voice hollowed by illness. I ate them? Is that what you thought you'd find?

He stood, shaky. I'm not an animal.

The man gathered items into a plastic grocery sack.

I can't fight you, he mumbled. I'm too sick. In went a brown teddy bear, a painted rattle with many spots worn through to wood.

In a way I'm glad you came. I can't care for them anymore. It's a lot of work.

The girl on the couch unfolded as if on cue and stretched like a dog, arching so far she slid off the cushion and onto her head. As Linda watched this, her stomach twisted.

She's yours, the man said. He peered at Linda's face, then at the girl. Clear as day.

The girl sat up, rubbed the spot she'd bruised.

Linda counted backward in her head. Beatrice was six.

She likes to walk, he said, as if explaining her hair. He thrust the bag into the girl's arms and nodded to the child seat. Grab that handle and hold tight. You're gonna help your mom get your brother home. She doesn't look like she can walk too steady.

Beatrice and the man stared at Linda, as if waiting for her to speak, or maybe just to leave.

Linda had expected something more dramatic. A struggle, maybe. She tightened her grip on her purse where the knife lay cozy in a rag. Something more than this. This, she imagined, was what it would feel like if she had to pick her kids up from a sitter she hated leaving them with. Aren't you going to apologize? she finally asked.

The man laughed, but not meanly. For what? It's just how I am. And I did right by them. He placed a hand on Beatrice's head and smiled down at her. What does an owl say, girl?

Beatrice cocked her head. Hoo hoo. Hoo hoo, she called, slow and serious.

Correct, the man said, and hobbled past Linda. She followed him into a dining room stuffed with tables made from plywood across sawhorses, a few appliances lining the walls. The tables stretched in rows, benches flanking each. It looked like a cafeteria, and easily could seat a hundred.

Photos of the man with different children covered the plywood walls. In one he was a young man helping a small boy hold up a fish almost as long as the boy was tall. The boy showed hugely gapped teeth, and the man himself was caught midlaugh. In another, the man, older, stood in front of the house, before all the serpentine additions. Gathered around him, in one big hug, were children of all ages, maybe forty in all. Everyone smiled. Between the poster boards were tacked wrinkled, aged letters. *Dear Dad*, they all began. Taped to some were pictures of other families, and Linda understood that these children had become adults and wrote home to the man as any child would write home to a father. But did the pictures show their own families, or ones they had stolen from whatever neighborhood they now lived behind? Had they grown up to be like the man? Or were they just regular people?

She watched the man stoop into one of the refrigerators and fill a tote bag with apples. He was mostly bald, with drooping ears and gnarled elbows. He looked so much older than he had in her yard, though that was only a few months ago. He creaked back upright and walked the bag of apples over to her.

And of course you'll take the others, he said. Then, already lost in his own nostalgia, he murmured, My children.

o o o

Through the woods, Linda led a procession of strange little faces of varying ages, the bigger ones carrying the crawlers. Each time she tried to count them, they muddled and mixed themselves. She thought there were at least a couple dozen. They were all smudged with dirt and smelled like a horde.

Beatrice walked beside Linda, swinging Lewis's chair wildly. The girl should look familiar, but Linda thought her the strangest of all. She watched Linda out of the corner of her eye, and seemed ready to flinch should Linda reach for her. So Linda didn't.

As they left the house, many of the children, crying, had embraced the man, and he had cried too. Most called him Dad, but she heard a few call him Kevin. *Kevin*, she repeated to herself, and she almost laughed at how ordinary it all began to seem. At the head of the trail the man had worn through the woods, Linda looked back. The man was slumped on the porch, already yellow and dead.

What if the man hadn't been ill? Would he have fought her for the children? Linda wasn't sure anymore. Perhaps he'd never intended to keep them, to become caretaker to untold numbers of children throughout his life. Maybe he'd had other plans but long ago had given in to a sick impulse. And the defeated young women thought this must be what motherhood is, and they let it continue. They learned to expect—and so, accept—certain losses. And the man waited a lifetime for some relief.

Linda regarded her sullen brood. They stood expectant, sad and hungry-looking. Her stomach sank.

○ ○ ○

Linda phoned her neighbors and left messages. The man is dead, and I have all the children. Come and see if any are yours.

Only a few women came, called out names that weren't recognized, tentatively lifted children, peered at their heads and bottoms as if making sure of something, then left with the ones that most fit what they thought they remembered or what they most wanted. Only one woman teared up with joy. The others emanated a feeling more like confusion. Or resignation. If you could suddenly get back everything you'd already said good-bye to, would you want it? Other women she had called answered with their silence. They never came.

Linda recognized their parents in some of them. Inherited noses, eyes, smiles, temperaments, gave them away. She was certain she could match these children, walk them over to their proper homes. Two children who had earlier been claimed reappeared on her doorstep, apology notes pinned to their jackets. She could have sent them back to their indecisive parents. But she didn't do it. She kept all the children.

Linda hired men to build a cramped addition onto the house, and her husband worked extra hours to pay for it and for all their new expenses. Often after work he took long night drives, drank late at a bar, anything to avoid coming home to this new bustling clan. Linda remembered how, when they were newly married and fantasizing about their family to come, he had argued that three was the ideal number of children. Now they had twenty-five.

The new addition covered the footprint of the backyard and left no room for outside play. The children slept in rows on rough-hewn bunk beds that reminded her of a ship's galley: industrial, sad, adult. She tried not to picture it that way and concentrated instead on how these children were no longer stolen. They had been found. Freed. She had rescued them. But was anything better? Her husband was unhappy; the children who had seemed content in their forest home now seemed lethargic. And though she had her children back, she still felt grief for what could have been, for what would never be. Maybe this is what her neighbors had tried to tell her. Motherhood was naturally replete with loss.

She tried to keep her own children close. She put their beds in her bedroom. For Lewis a crib and then later his own small bed, with a train engine's face painted onto the foot, covered in conductor-striped sheets. And for Beatrice—a bed with pink sheets and a comforter trimmed with lace. But Beatrice didn't sleep there.

Beatrice prowled the house at night, looking through cabinets and books. She went for long walks and came back with things that didn't belong to her. In the morning, Linda would find her curled in a corner under a moldy, yellowed blanket Linda didn't recognize and couldn't remember bringing from the man's house. Beatrice's socks would be half off her feet in that way socks slide off children's feet but never adults'.

Beatrice kept her treasures in her corner of the living room, and at night, when the children were in bed, when Lewis was asleep, when her husband was working late to avoid the teeming house, when Beatrice was loping through the halls, Linda explored the collection. Mixed in with the dirty baseballs and lost car keys, Linda found a box of letters she had written to her stolen daughter and hoped one day to give to her. Baby pictures were tucked into a dog-eared grief book heavily marked with Linda's handwriting. Beneath it, Linda's hairbrush, full of wiry grays, a sweater she hadn't worn in years, a swatch of pink snipped from Beatrice's own lonely bedding doused in an expensive perfume Linda kept on her dresser.

Linda waited for some warm tug of emotion, but the collection only made her uneasy. This study in the past cast doubt in Linda's mind about the girl—she couldn't possibly be Beatrice; Linda felt little for her. At times she wondered if the man had lied to her, or mistaken this girl for another. When the children were all together, Linda watched the girls and tried to feel a yearning for them, something. She asked herself, Is that how my Beatrice would look at age six? But none of them were like the daughter she'd spent years building in her imagination. And neither was this interloper who always seemed unsure where to stand, with her sly stare and twigs in her hair.

Some nights, after Beatrice had slipped out, Linda stood at the door and placed her hand on the lock, debated turning it. What would become of her? Linda pictured the girl returning to the sprawling house in the woods where she'd been raised, where her hiding spots were, padding across those bare floors with her dirty feet, tacking up new pictures, living like the man, collecting things in her travels, which would eventually lead to collecting children.

These were rare times Linda felt a straightforward, understandable emotion for Beatrice. She felt pity for the girl who was far from home. But it wasn't the same as love.

So she took to imagining Beatrice truly roaming, undetected, wild; able to cast off the trappings of her true home and Linda's home. Searching for a new home in the bottom of a dead tree, or maybe in a wet cave deep within a park. She'd sleep on pine boughs in the hot summer and shiver in her filthy yellow blanket in the winter.

Linda spent long nights composing Beatrice's adventures, obsessing over the details. She tried to convince herself they had the makings of an enviable childhood: Beatrice drinking from fountains and bathing in lakes, calling owls at night and chasing butterflies during the day, hiding from snooping dogs, raiding squirrel stashes, spying on crows, making speeches to the tallest trees, weaving weeds through her hair, drawing pictures on sidewalks with burned wood, being a princess, reading street signs like they were adventure stories, laughing with ducks who told her jokes, digging through garbage, watching, from a tree, happy families picnicking across a great lawn, and waiting for the moment when she might slip unnoticed among them as though she belonged to them and steal their lunches, then, more.

GIRL ON GIRL

Freshman year starts, and somehow everyone is someone else, someone older, someone interested in the faraway future life. Everyone except me. I'm back from a summer at my dad's divorce condo—decorated to seem remote and armed—and no one cares. I'm watching my old clique grind into boys on the dance floor while the male coaches-slash-civics-teachers roughly separate them, swipe at inappropriate girl parts, and get away with it in the authoritative heat of the moment. I'm watching it all, cringing, but I wish I were in the scrum.

I want to be fondled. I want someone to press me some-where too hard. I'm hot with shame. The good kind.

I turn to Clara. She never talks because her parents are professors. She still wears girls' undershirts, and she can't quit horses. She looks about as far away from the dance as a dead star.

"What do you think Mr. Ryan *tastes* like?"

Clara turns red. I do too.

My math teacher is breaking up a couple by getting in between them, his groin brushing a junior in a glitter skirt.

He has a chestnut beard and glassy eyes. Sharp shoulders. I'm imagining inspecting the pale skin under those fine dark hairs of his forearm as he leans over my desk to tell me what x is. He must taste like just-dug rocks. My mouth waters. His calculus fingers wiggle toward me. He says I'm a ripe pear. He is very close. My ears ring. Pears are rotten.

I smack my head to stop my dirty movie.

That's when I spot Marni tossing her hair around the way women do on daytime talk shows. She's screaming at her boyfriend, Mack. She's louder than the music, and it sounds like one long *wee*. Marni is attractive and fat, with an unnaturally narrow waist and unnaturally big boobs and ass. Her cheeks and lips are plump, but somehow her jaw is sharp, and she looks like a sexy Victorian porcelain doll. She wears her hair big and together it all works to make her seem normal-sized with a lot to grab. But I've seen her getting into her pajamas and I've seen her gullet a whole pizza at a birthday party, and there is nothing normal-sized about her. She is a magnificent cow. She was my best friend. I wrote her twenty-six letters this summer, and she wrote me none. We haven't talked since middle school.

Mack grabs some of that big hair. He pulls her to him, mouth wide, rooting for hers. Marni raises her hand. Maybe she'll stick fingers in there, swirl them around. I want her to. But she scratches at his face and hauls herself across the crowded floor. Couples part for her because somehow she is revered; rumor is she'll be at least nominated for homecoming, though she won't beat anyone on cheerleading. In the corner of the gym Theresa and Hill, Marni's new bests, detangle from their dates. They're getting felt up, but they somehow know Marni is on the move and they follow. I guess that's what it means to be bests now. I only know what's happening because I'm spying from bleacher land.

"I wonder what that was all about," I say to Clara. My voice is conspiratorial. I'm trying to make gossip. But the dead star barely shrugs.

My knee quivers like a compass needle.

I know Marni's favorite spot.

Dancing couples step all over me like I'm a cat underfoot. It takes me two whole songs to get across the gym. I throw my shoulder against the rusty door. It squawks.

The hallway is quiet but full of couples pressing against lockers. Skirts inch up thighs; pants creep low. I can't tell if it's just style or if they're all about to do *it*. Where are the teachers? What's that smell? I want to grab all their hair as I run, and give a terrific yank. I want to sweep their legs and watch them go down.

The girls' bathroom is a floor above, at the end of the hall. I hear thudding and I sprint up the stairs. The ruckus gets louder down the corridor. I hear a thump and then an *ooph*, another thump and an *ooph*. From behind the door Marni shrills, "Harder!" and it's like she's in my ear.

I crack the door and see Marni lying on the floor, coat spread under her, her hair splayed out. She looks romantic and princesslike, and then Theresa lands a socked foot hard onto Marni's protruding fat gut.

"Ooph." Marni's cherub face bunches. Hill stomps her size nines down. They both say, "Ooph," then Hill wheezes like it's hot.

"Come on," Marni growls. She reaches for Theresa's leg

just as Theresa lets it drop. Marni's head snaps back on the floor. A sick crunch.

I gasp. The three heads jolt. They see it's just me.

"What do you want, Fart?" Marni sneers.

She's lying there: beaten, regal. Cracks in the windows make shimmering webs. The heater is clanging. The stomping girls are huffing. Everyone is waiting. I want to join, is what I want. I want to land some full-force kicks. I want to miss and get her shoulder, her head. I want to jam a toothbrush down her throat, make her thin.

"You're going to get in trouble," I say. I try to sound loud and sarcastic, but I don't.

The girls exchange looks and laugh too loudly; one big fake *ha* each. It's effortlessly coordinated.

Theresa plants a foot on Marni's belly, claiming her like an explorer. "She's in trouble all right," she says, arching her back, sticking her gut out, rubbing it. She strains her face and moans.

Marni on Mack. Mack in Marni. A little Mack and Marni. My head rushes. I want to watch, hear the sounds.

Marni, a scowl storming, pushes Theresa, who topples down to the tile and stays down, plays dead.

"Get out," Marni roars at everyone, but I'm the one who runs.

Outside the gym, I find a gaggle of teachers gossiping. A flask is tucked when I skid up to them, breathless. I tell them Marni Duke is getting beat up in the second-floor girls'. I can't even tell them why. We're just fourteen.

I'm hot with shame. The stomach kind. The kind that hurts. I run home, punching low tree limbs as I go.

o o o

In homeroom on Monday, everyone whispers about a fight in the girls' bathroom. The rumor is Marni. The rumor is one girl held her down while another kicked her. People gasp. *Marni from Homecoming?* Coos of sympathy all around.

I'm summoned to the office.

Marni, Theresa, and Hill slouch in the lobby, and the principal calls me in. The girls glare as I close the door.

He asks, "Gabby, what did you see?"

They glare through glass, and I can't speak until the principal lowers the blinds. As they fall, Hill raises a fist. I catch Marni's eye, and it's an eye so familiar I'm momentarily grateful to have its attention. Then the blinds are down. It's just me.

The principal wants my version.

"I don't have a version," I say.

He sighs. "Just tell me what you saw."

I tell him what I saw—Marni on the ground, Hill and Theresa stomping.

"Where?" he asks.

I touch my stomach, watch him jot on a notepad. "But I ran," I say. "I don't know anything else."

"Did they say anything to you?"

I shake my head no. I can't say.

He stares, pen poised.

I clear my throat, speak sideways. "Marni had a fight with her boyfriend right before. You could talk to him?"

The principal is confused. "Was he there?"

The swirl pattern of the carpet is moving; it wants to crawl up my leg. I shake my head again. "No."

"And how do you know about this fight?"

I shrug and look at my hands, the skinny fingers and fat tips. They're like frog hands; sticky, creepy. They'd ruin a lily pad. I smooth my strained jeans. Something smells. I'm sure it's me.

"I watched them," I answer.

The principal nods, leafs through a file of papers—the paper version of me.

I'm dismissed.

I brace myself for the lobby, for the baseball bat I'm sure will meet my skull when I enter it, but Marni and the girls are gone.

I walk to the nurse's office and puke on her desk. She sends me home. I go the backyard route so no one will see me.

∘ ∘ ∘

In homeroom Tuesday, everyone whispers about how there was no fight between Marni and Hill and Theresa. People nod. *They're bests, you know.* Who lied? The rumor is me. "Gabby," girls whisper conspiratorially, ready to hate. "Who?" Uncertain glances from desk to desk. "Gabrielle?" Heads shake. No recognition. I'm sitting right there.

I'm in line for lunch and Theresa comes up behind me, digs her plastic tray into my spine. I double over my ravioli.

"Meet Marni out front before fifth. Do it," she bleats.

I sit next to Clara. Her whole look is skeptical. I don't touch my food. The ten-minute bell.

"Clara," I hiss. "Come to the bathroom."

She startles like I've just woken her. Looking out the window is her form of sleep. But she follows.

First-floor bathroom. Lots of postlunch traffic. I peer under doors. The so-what smokers are enshrouded near the sinks. My eyes water.

I grab Clara's hand, but she takes it away quickly, disturbed. Too close, she seems to say. I think I hate her. "Just stand guard outside the bathroom, okay? When the bell rings, text if you see Marni, Hill, or Theresa."

"Why? Because you lied?"

How does Clara know a rumor? She's a corner-sitter. "I didn't lie. Just do it."

I lock myself behind a stall door and crouch on the toilet. I can monitor through the crack. I wait.

Girls rush in, rake brushes through their hair, apply shiny gloss with wands, blot, spit into sinks. Cheap perfumes mist the air.

The bell rings; the room clears out. A drip glugs down a drain.

I text Clara a question mark, but I get no response. She's probably wandered into some empty classroom to wait for her life to begin.

The door swings open. I smell Marni before I hear her, the fake coconut of her sunless tan. Hill and Theresa stifle awful snorting *haws*. They walk the line of stalls, kick in each door. They're not wondering where I am. They know. I make myself into a small clump on the toilet seat. The whoosh of the door parts my bangs.

Hill pulls me out. "Nice try," she mocks.

From behind the cracked door, Clara peeks. We lock

eyes. I wait for a mouthed apology. She scans the scene and, incredibly, smiles before bolting. Have a nice day. I hate her.

Hill and Theresa each pull an arm behind my back. Marni smiles and knees me in the groin so hard I dry heave. They scoot to avoid my puke, but when it doesn't come, Marni knees me again.

"Ooph," I say and gasp for air. I'm not big like Marni. I'm misshapen, weak. My legs are logs, but my middle is bird bones, doughy, and her knee reaches the center of me.

I'm bent. Hill and Theresa try to pull me up but I pull down, not out of preservation or show of strength but out of defeat. I want to hug the ground. My legs tremble. Marni's hands reach for my face and I let them guide me gently up because they're her hands. I know their gentleness from when she taught me things, placed my fingers on guitar strings to press as she strummed, held me up on a bike. When she soothed me after my dad left. I look into her eyes and at her sweet, pink face. She wears more makeup now, and under all the coconut she smells stale, as though she smokes outside so that the smoke will blow away but it gets caught in all that hair. For a moment I think she's going to smile, rub a smudge from my cheek, kiss me. But then, finally, her fist meets my face. I hear the crack, and now it's the floor reaching for me. I see their smiles as I go.

Lying here, what I cry about is that not one of them speaks as they leave. There's nothing to say about the downfall of unremarkable me. The only sounds are their different shoes on the tile: the click of too-grown-up heels, scuff of sneakers, clomp of daunting boots. They strut out the whining door and down the hallway, uncaringly late for fifth.

The tile is cool. Dirt shames my cheek. I have a bug's-eye view of the bathroom floor, littered with snarls of long girl hair and dropped cigarette ash. A glittery popped-off stick-on nail lies almost close enough to touch.

o o o

I wake up in bed. My head hurts. I can't breathe right. A rigid thing covers my nose. I tenderly pick. Crusty blood clogs my nostrils. I try to drink from a glass of water but the nose won't let me.

The door creaks. Mom's tentative head appears. Her eyes crinkle above her nervous smile.

"Oh good, you're awake." She perches at the edge of my bed, smoothes the hair across my forehead, and then I'm aware that I have a bump there.

"What happened?" I gurgle.

Her hand stops in mom alarm. "Don't you remember?"

"Yes."

The hand continues across my forehead. "Do you want to tell me who did this?"

"No."

The hand stops, rests heavily on the protruding bump. It hurts. Does she know she's hurting me? I think she does.

"I mean, I don't remember. I mean, I don't know."

Mom sighs, disappointed. "Okay for now, Gabrielle. But we're not done." Then she brightens like she's just been handed pages for the next scene. She says, "You have a visitor!" She straightens the sheet across my chest. "Honey, Marni is here."

I tense. "Why?"

She smiles self-pityingly. Her daughter is strange. "To see you. To see if you're okay. Isn't that nice?" She pauses. "Marni hasn't been by in such a long time. I didn't think you two were still friends."

"We're not."

"Well, then, it's doubly nice that she came, isn't it? Are you up for it?" She's up for it, I can tell. She's already fondling the doorknob.

I remember how Marni's fist cut the smoky light shining through the cracked windows of that bathroom. It's half-the-day-left light. It's the kind of light here now.

I nod, and when Mom leaves, I pull myself up to a sit.

Marni tiptoes in, straight-backed and calm, her face friendly and serene. For a moment, I'm relieved. But when the door clicks behind, her body slouches into a threat. Hands on her hips. She looks at my face and snorts. "You look like shit."

"Did you come to apologize?"

Her guffaw is from Drama. "No."

"Did you get suspended?"

She guffaws again. "Why would I? We didn't do anything wrong. They were helping me. It's what friends do."

I flinch. What a jab. "Then why are you here?" I'm acting tough.

Marni squeezes her hands together and looks around the room, everywhere but at me. She shrugs. "It didn't work," she says with fake indifference. "I need it to work. And now Terry and Hilly are spooked." My stomach tightens at the nicknames, the intimacy. "That's your fault, you know. So."

"So what?" I yell it just enough, but not enough for Mom to hear, wherever she is.

"Finish it," she yells back in the same way, but meaner.

"Why me? Why not Mack?"

Marni looks at me, disgusted, like I'm a horror under my fresh, flowery sheets. "I thought you were my friend." Her chin quivers, and even though I know the logic here is wrong in that way that I almost choke on, I don't care.

"I am."

She waits for me to prove it.

But I concentrate on the feeling of air through my nose, in and out to slow the anticipation growing in my stomach.

"Fine," Marni hisses. "Then I'll do it myself." She punches at her gut, her fists cluttered with cheap rings, barely denting her fat inner tube, hysterical.

"Stop," I plead, and grab her hands. "You know that won't work."

She looks at me.

"I have to step on it."

Marni nods.

o o o

I make a soft bed on the floor with my comforter and the quilt my grandmother fumbled her way through. It's how I used to make Marni's bed for sleepovers. She lies down; I cradle her head, place a pillow under it. Stretch her hair out around her like she's floating in a pond. I know the pillowcase will smell of coconut after. I know I will let the scent fade on its own before I'll wash it.

I fold her hands over her chest like she's a dead person,

and I see the slivers of scum under her nails. It's the dirt from dirty things. It's Mack's back skin from scratching. She never cleans. Is that even how it works? I'm salivating.

"What's it feel like?" I ask, because even though she has stopped liking me, she's the only person who can tell me.

Marni rolls her eyes. I want to slap her hard, but I have no one else to ask. Does it feel slick like glue? Is it a pressure like shoving? I picture my dad's girl calendar, tacked on the stainless steel fridge. I can't ask him. I can't ask my mom. I can't ask Clara because I hate her, and what would she know?

Marni bites her lip thoughtfully, and I almost think she's going to tell me, but then her face scrunches like she's going to cry, just for a second. "Just do it," she orders and punches my shin.

I drop my knee with what feels like my whole weight behind. It sinks into her like I'm landing on Mom's too-soft bed.

"Ooph," she bellows.

"Shh. You're being too loud," I whisper. "Why can't you just go to the doctor?"

The way she looks at me, I can't figure out if there is something about the world I don't know yet, or the other way around. There's something about the world that isn't real to her yet, either, like doctors, or problems with simple solutions. The world is where things feel too hard to explain, and so they stay a secret.

I drop my knee again.

"Oh, oh," she moans, and I worry Mom will hear.

"Shut up," I snap. I feel the sharp shame of being in

trouble even though no one knows. It was always this way with Marni—thrills and pains. I always felt good and bad because of her. I shove her hard with my foot. "You're trouble."

She gasps, and then really sobs. "You're so mean."

"I'm mean?"

"You're the meanest!"

I didn't think I was mean. I thought Marni was mean. Were we mean together? And if we used to be mean together, why couldn't we still be? I want to be meanest with her.

I find a pair of balled-up socks on the floor and push them into Marni's mouth. She makes protest sounds and starts to take them out, but I push them in farther until she gags. She quiets down and watches me with big, alert eyes.

I prod my toe into the fattest part, just below her belly button. I step there lightly with my bare foot; steady myself with the bedpost. I place the other foot. It's like being in an inflatable castle at a street fair; everywhere I step gives way, and it's hard to get my balance. My foot slips, rakes her side. She winces. I finally get on good, hand on the bedpost, other arm outstretched. Balanced. Her belly squishes under my feet, but beneath all that fat is a small, hard mound that seems to push up against my weight in self-defense.

I begin to bounce up and down, lightly, and Marni huffs quietly into those socks, to the rhythm I make. With each bounce, I gain momentum like I'm on a trampoline, and so I bounce a little harder, faster. I'm no longer slipping. Marni's huffs get louder and I dig my heels in as a warning. She squeals unhappily through the socks, and after that, the only noise she makes is a tiny gurgle in her throat like she's going to vomit.

It's like the fat has melted away, and all I can really feel now is that secret mound. I want to break it open, slay the dragon, save the princess. I don't want to stop until I'm sure it has worked.

Tears flow from Marni's eyes; they run through her hair, pool in her ears, spread darkly on the pillowcase. Her balled fists unclench, and she covers her face.

I can't explain it, but I feel maybe the best I've felt since the end of last year, when on the last day of school me and Marni and a couple other girls snuck into movies all day without getting caught. We'd heard it could be done from someone's older sister. We'd leave before the end of one movie, run into the bathroom, and hide in stalls to wait for the next one; me and Marni squatting in the same stall, feet on the toilet seat, leaning against the walls, laughing into our hands at the fact that we were doing the things other kids did. We were becoming like other kids. And it was so easy. Just a series of steps.

MAN V. NATURE

It had been days since Phil and his two oldest friends drunkenly fished from the middle of the great lake for fat trout, the sweet orange flesh of which tasted best grilled over charcoal, under stars tossed absurdly across the sky like birdseed.

Days since Phil's boat ran out of gas, stranding him and his friends during this, their annual fishing trip.

Days since Phil had seen another boat or passing tanker, which was strange on a lake usually choked by commercial traffic and sport boats.

Days since they'd placed bets on a timetable for rescue, and grown bored of spitting contests, of swapping sex stories, of imaginary card games.

Days since they'd devoured the beer brats and the buns. The coal-cooked sweet potatoes. The breakfast eggs. The butter for frying. The three bloody steaks they'd brought for the last night, when they figured they'd be tired of fish. All the A-1.

Days since Dan claimed the water was safe to drink,

even though they were shitting and pissing into it, saying, "It dilutes," as he swished a turd away.

Days since Ross, standing at the prow like a hood ornament, shielded his eyes against the bronze water of sunrise and insisted he saw land through a retreating fog, while their large pleasure craft heaved, weighty and useless on the swells.

Looking back, it's clear they'd been fevered by exposure, buoyed by assumptions, not to mention drunk, when they decided to abandon said thirty-foot pleasure craft—the one thing Phil had held on to in the divorce, with its comfortable sleeping cabin and mini-fridge still stocked with two dozen beers—to jump into the cramped rubber lifeboat. They'd cheered, certain they could navigate it to a shore Ross insisted was there. "We'll be walking on the beach in an hour. I just know it," he'd said. They'd sat straight-backed and high-kneed like kings on tricycles; they rowed like ecstatics.

But that was days ago.

○ ○ ○

Ross and Dan, tired out from rowing nowhere, rubbed their tender shoulders and watched Phil with what he thought was skepticism, but hoped was appreciation, after he swore he could row them to land by himself, *No problem,* with the two child-sized oars—cast-offs from a summer camp and covered in green chipped paint.

"I've *got* this," Phil said reassuringly. "I've been in worse shit." He'd been an army man, after all. Ross and Dan exchanged a look. What did the look mean? Phil felt nervous.

It was a risk to take charge. He used to like risk. But lately he'd grown wary of it.

Was the boat moving? With no landmark, Phil couldn't say. He strained harder.

"Remember how I was the star of our high school team?" Phil reminded, hoping to bolster their faith in him, with his quivering shoulders and hands wet with panic.

Ross said, "Of track."

Dan scoffed, "And field." Phil was tall and skinny, had an abnormally long stride but not much strength.

Ross and Dan laughed. It was the first genuine laugh Phil had heard since they'd been relaxing in their real boat. The only sounds since had been waves slapping the rubber lifeboat, an occasional bird whining past. They conversed softly, as if to use their regular voices would be too jarring in such small quarters. *"Can you pass some jerky?"* in a whisper. The response, not necessarily unkind. *"No. You had your piece today."*

Ross and Dan's laugh sounded like a new thing, so Phil joined in. It felt good to laugh.

"Dan the man," he said with affection. He clamped his hand on Dan's shoulder. It felt so normal; even Dan's bristling at his touch.

Ross and Dan hunkered into an exhausted sleep while Phil tried to row his friends to shore.

In the night rains came, and the men groggily scooped water from around their feet until it began to merely drizzle and they drooped back into an unhappy sleep.

When morning came, Phil held only one oar.

Had he fallen asleep? the two men asked Phil. Yes, yes,

DIANE COOK

he had, he answered. Hadn't he tied the oars to his wrists so he wouldn't drop them while he slept? Like they'd all agreed they would? they cried. No, he answered calmly, no, he hadn't.

Phil cleared his throat. "This is not a problem," he said. Phil would row with the one oar into the currents that moved like ribbons through the water. The currents would help push them closer to the shore. Gray lake and sky blended into a perfectly blank dome. If someone told them they were upside down, Phil thought, he would not be surprised. When Dan and Ross chewed their lips and exchanged more looks, Phil decided, they are putting their faith in me.

The boat dragged in circles. And when the weather broke and blue sky emerged, the men discovered that the land Ross swore he'd seen—that Dan and Phil believed he'd seen—was gone; the horizon lay sharp in all directions. If something had been seen, Phil guessed it had been clouds, a bank of them hugging the water like a real distant shore would.

Ross pawed at his face and sobbed, "My girls," for his wife, Bren, and their three daughters, who were sure to have called the police by now, who'd no doubt sent search parties, search boats, search planes. Which made it even more frustrating that the men were still lost, drifting, alone. Phil looked at Ross's sunburned, bald head, handed over his own hat, and said gently, "Hey, boss, you're blistering."

o o o

Each morning they rotated positions, two on the plastic bench in back and one on the rubber bottom at the bow.

The two on the bench bumped elbows, smelled the other all day, shifted ass cheeks to avoid sores. Whoever sat on the bottom could stretch his legs and lean against the side. They coveted the spot for sleeping. Early on, Phil had hoped the other men would offer the spot to him indefinitely; he was the tallest, which made folding himself onto the plastic bench that much harder. Plus, it was his boat. But the other men decided to share. It was more fair. In return for getting the spot for the day, the man on the bottom had to massage cramps out of the other men's calves and feet.

Phil was stretched out, locking and unlocking his knees. Quietly, he kneaded the blood back into Ross's bloated legs while Ross groaned in good pain. Dan twirled his mustache and stared into nothing, patiently awaiting his turn. Though they weren't on the ocean, all around them Phil smelled salted air. It must be coming from us, he thought, and licked his own shoulder. He tasted like a warm olive. His mouth watered precious spit.

The thirty-foot pleasure craft was long gone. After that first day of rowing, they could still see it as night fell, bobbing on the horizon like a fishing lure. But in the morning the sun lit flat, empty water, with no pleasure craft in sight. That was a hard morning for Phil. The men asked him to use the GPS to find out where they were. And Phil had to admit that it was still on the boat they'd abandoned; he'd forgotten to grab it, he'd said.

The truth was Phil *had* remembered it but couldn't unhook it from the control panel, and really had never learned how to use it anyway. He only took the boat out this one week a year. It had sat in a marina weathering while he was living out west. He wasn't even sure why he'd fought Patricia so hard for it. Maybe because she had wanted it, which was ridiculous after she had given him so much grief for buying it in the first place. "Get a job you like," she'd barked. "Then you won't have to fill your empty life with meaningless crap like that stupid boat." He cried when he saw the boat in the list of assets she demanded. Now she had the house, the nicer car, the dog, which she gave away to an old friend. The friend had called Phil to offer the dog back, saying it felt weird, owning Phil's dog. But Phil didn't know how to go about retrieving the dog. He'd gone east, and the dog was west. He didn't want to fly to get the dog and be in the same city as Patricia—there was the issue of that court order. But he didn't know how to ship a dog. Would he have to call an airline to schedule it? UPS? The thought of making phone calls overwhelmed him. So the friend kept the dog.

"He's asleep," Dan garbled, and nudged Phil's hands onto his own leg. "My turn."

The three men had been babies together in the same neighborhood; their moms took turns watching them, shuttling them from house to house without ever having to cross a busy street. Still, Dan and Ross had always been the better friends; they were true next-door neighbors, while Phil lived down the street. They flashed Morse-code messages through their bedroom windows when they should have been sleeping. But Phil was too far away to join. Ross and Dan went to the local university, Phil to the army. But they all stayed friends, Phil made sure. Dan was a television writer in the city, a serial dater, the best man at their weddings. Ross lived in their hometown, had the family, golfed at the municipal golf course. Phil atrophied at a base out west, met and married Patricia there, then stayed to be with her. What a mistake. That kept him out of the loop. He should have tried to come back home. Dan's parents still lived in town, and Phil knew Dan visited often. Ross and Dan must have seen each other then, but they never talked about it.

One time, a couple days into their lifeboat drift, Phil had jumped into the water to cool off after assurances from Dan and Ross that they would help him back in. A few yards from the lifeboat, he turned to watch them. He saw how the men stretched out luxuriously, how Ross clasped his hands behind his head and sighed, and how Dan did the same. The men smiled and laughed about something, enjoying themselves, almost. Phil never left the boat again.

o o o

Days passed. The men hadn't spoken in at least two. Or was it more? How many more days? Phil wondered. As another night fell, his mind droned. He hated being alone with it.

"Gentlemen," he said, "Let's play a game."

"Like playing imaginary cards?" Dan scoffed.

"Sure," Phil said gamely. "That might be good."

"I was joking," Dan said.

"Okay." Phil tried again. "We could bet on if we'll get rescued."

Ross scowled. "You're a macabre fuck."

Phil fake chuckled. "You're right. How stupid of me. That's not a game." He stroked his chin. "What about girls? We haven't talked about them in a while. That can't be bad, can it?"

The other men shrugged.

"Ross, why don't you start," Phil encouraged.

"Fine."

Phil closed his eyes. He was just beginning to stiffen when Ross stopped talking and yawned pointedly.

"This is boring," he said. "Also, I'm tired." His blisters had turned to wet sores, and he winced every time the wind stroked his oozing bald head. His energy bled out of it.

"You're always tired," Phil said. "Keep talking." Even with his eyes closed, Phil could tell looks were exchanged— the boat shifted slightly as the men turned their heads.

In the distance, geese landed in a mess of honks and splashes. Ross remained quiet.

"Maybe just start from later in college," Phil said. He wanted to hear about Bren. Beautiful blond Bren.

Ross trudged through the story of the flexible roller skater and her bleached pubic hair, his voice flat and uninterested.

Phil waited.

"Then I met Bren," Ross said, and he choked on her name, sounding angry almost, which in a strange way made it a new story to Phil. Like a new encounter. A new first time. Nothing boring about that, Phil thought, his body warming.

There it was.

Ross sobbed into his clenched fist, unable to continue. But it was enough. Phil carefully slid his hand under his waistband, skimming the raw chafed skin around his middle, and tried to let the images and a light touch do the work so the boat wouldn't quiver. Sweet Bren wearing only cotton panties, giggling into her hand. He'd meant only to comfort himself, not climax, but he was the hardest thing for miles. Inside, everything lined up.

"We know what you're doing, Phil," Dan said, disgusted.

"Shut up," Phil hissed. Distracted, a banal dribble slipped out. But that was all. No big release. Frustrated tears sprang. "I hate you," he muttered. It sounded like a yell.

Phil hid behind his closed eyes. When he opened them, he saw that Dan was asleep, his head loose and lolling with the swells. But Ross sat rigid, arms crossed, his gaze seemingly fixed on Phil. In the shadows made from slivered moonlight, Phil couldn't tell if Ross's eyes were shut or if his stare was meant to accuse Phil of something. He held his breath. Soon, he heard Ross snore.

Even though Phil had the floor, he couldn't sleep. His inner drone continued. As night passed he watched the stars blur and the eerie green auroras appear, spilling along the horizon like paint. As his sight adjusted, the night was not as pitch-black as before. It shone through his eyelids like the glare from a streetlamp.

He picked at his crusty shorts. He filtered through questions to soothe himself to sleep. Why hadn't they been rescued? Where were the other boats? Was it the end of the world? What did Ross really think of him? Who did Dan like better? Every question he asked yielded an unsatisfying answer that woke him more. To make himself feel better, he ate the last of the peanuts. Then he leaned toward Dan, felt Dan's rotten sleep breath in his face, and cleanly plucked the last strip of jerky from his pocket.

o o o

Phil woke to the wind in his hair and Ross and Dan bellowing, "One, two, one, two!" They synchronized feeble hand scoops through the water like a crew team, but they went nowhere. They spun in slow circles.

Ross and Dan spat words and dusty saliva toward Phil. They'd woken disoriented, frenzied, lost to time.

"The jerky is gone!" Ross barked.

"The peanuts!" Dan screamed. He took a breath and screamed again.

The remaining oar was also gone.

"How?" Phil asked.

Ross and Dan stopped mid scoop.

"Someone must have taken it," Dan said, and scratched his palms, pilling bits of grime and skin. He looked over his shoulder as if someone had tapped it.

"Who could have done that?" Phil asked. He focused on seeming innocent.

Ross eyed him suspiciously.

There was no good answer to this question, and so they settled into an uneasy calm.

Phil felt roller-coaster queasy; the final part, when the hills come too quickly.

We are unlucky, he thought. Like people who always miss the bus, even with a schedule. Though maybe luck is cyclical. Maybe luck was constantly on the move, gracing people and then leaving them. People with luck or good fortune early in life—they'll crash into a snowbank and freeze to death, slowly over days, to the sound of other cars passing just out of sight, or get snarled in the propeller of a boat when they're snorkeling on a relaxing vacation, or die giving birth to their child. Phil tried to think of when luck had visited him last, if ever. Was he due for some, or had he squandered his share long ago?

o o o

Phil peered sheepishly at Ross from under his lashes. "I slept with your wife."

"I know." Ross dunked his head in the lake.

Dan clapped his hands gleefully, and the resulting pop was the morning's only other noise. "If I were a television writer, I'd be writing all this down, because this is *gold*."

"Dan, you *are* a television writer," Phil said. He laughed, but the lake dampened the sound and it came off morose.

Dan scowled. "That's what I *meant*. I *meant* if I had a pen." He picked at a sun blister on his thigh until he let loose the pus. He dabbed his finger and licked it.

"*Did* you sleep with my wife?" Ross asked, easing a leg out for a stretch. It brushed by Phil's shoulder, purposefully, Phil thought.

Ross dunked his hands into the lake and gave each underarm a good scrub. He smelled them with fascination.

"Does it matter?" Phil asked. He'd hoped what he said would come off as a joke, and was annoyed it hadn't.

"Yeah. Yeah, I think it actually does, now that you mention it." Ross flicked his wet hands in Phil's face. "Now that we're here, I think it matters."

"Well, then, no, I didn't."

"Why did you say you did?"

"Because I *wanted* to. I've always *wanted* to sleep with your wife. She was hot."

Dan nodded. "She *is* hot."

Ross shrugged and twirled the minute hand around and around on his watch.

Phil scratched his head. "Why did you say 'I know' when I said I slept with her, if I never slept with her?" He was beginning to suspect Bren had said something to Ross. It was years ago, and they'd been so drunk, and it was only a blow job.

"Because I thought you did. I always thought you did."

"How could you think that? How could you think I'd do that to you?"

"Because I banged your sister. Remember?"

"Why would you bring that up? When we get home I *am* going to sleep with Bren. You deserve it." Phil stared out at the water. The way it moved on its own made him feel vaguely wet, like he was becoming part of the lake, being absorbed.

Ross chuckled. "No chance," he said, not even bothering to look at Phil. Which stung. Did he mean they had no chance of making it home, Phil wondered, or that he had no chance with Bren? How could Ross seem so sure? *Had* Bren said something? Phil squirmed in the bottom of the boat, trying to quell his burgeoning erection. He wanted to sleep with Bren badly.

"If I were writing this into a television sitcom," Dan mused, "or even a movie, I would have written this as a fight scene. Every time you guys say something, I'd have you start wrestling, so that the boat is almost tipping, and things get very tense for the audience, which thinks the boat *is* going to tip, but then I, or, you know, the actor playing me, intervenes and says something like—" Dan put his finger to his lips, thinking, then hollered, " 'Hey fellas, something something blah blah,' and then cue laugh track"—he pointed to the wavy gray horizon—"and that would calm you down because, you know, metaphors, etc. And then some action music would play, and we'd start figuring a way out of this mess."

Phil looked at Ross. He wiggled his eyebrows in a way that asked, *Is he losing it?* But Ross wouldn't look at him.

Ross, instead, looked at Dan with interest. "What *is* the way out of this mess?"

Dan scratched at the rubber seams beneath him. "I'm glad you finally asked. Let's flag down one of the tankers we keep seeing."

"We haven't seen any tankers," Phil said.

Dan's face registered shock, but then a vague smile appeared.

Ross glared at Phil.

"All right, then," Ross said soothingly to Dan, "we're three men in a boat in a large lake that is a major shipping route. Why have no boats passed to rescue us? I want you to write me a world in which that happens. I want my own television show, dammit."

So Dan told them about how, the other day, a coup d'état occurred in Canada. Rebels blocked all waterways and ports in protest, and were holding the prime minister hostage. Armed gunmen had broken into his room late at night while he enjoyed a cigar and a brandy, though this particular boutique hotel had strict no-smoking rules, which would be communicated by a slow pan from a No Smoking sign to the prime minister relishing a thick exhale just before the armed men barged in, threw a bag over his head, and dragged him through the hallway to the service elevator. Patrons screamed and cowered against walls at the sight of the guns because Canadians are peaceful nancies. The armed men brought the prime minister to the basement, which was really a dungeon from colonial times. They tied him to a chair and threatened to rape his daughters if he didn't cooperate. They're twins. "Double the pleasure," one of the more dastardly gunmen said, twirling his waxed mustache. The prime minister broke under the pressure of picturing his beautiful brunette daughters brutally raped, shown in slow, soft-lit vignettes so that it's classy and, of course, feminist. As viewers, we'd be horrified and so we would all understand—we would *have sympathy for*—the prime minister when he handed over the country to these armed men.

Dan paused, finger to lips again, and again looked over his shoulder at an imagined encroaching someone or something. He continued in a whisper. "Okay, listen, the army steps in, overthrows the prime minister, strips him of the authority to give the country to the gunmen, and proceeds to battle the counterforces laying siege to all of the rebel territories. So there are no boats here right now because in the seaway that leads to the ocean, the one we're heading for, a fantastic battle is taking place. Picture it: Underwater torpedoes! Cannons! They're fired from the bluffs by scrappy yet handsome, thrown-together village armies. Your run-of-the-mill believe-in-able poor-people types. The kind that wear potato-sack clothes and such. Somehow a pod of government-trained beluga whales is unleashed to deliver explosives—strapped to their heads on helmets, okay—by swimming under enemy boats and blowing up themselves *and* the boats. Total kamikaze shit. We're talking whale medal of honor." Dan punched the air. "The war is on. Boom. Prime time."

"That's quite a show," Ross said admiringly. "What are you going to call it?"

Dan snapped his fingers. "*Man V. Nature.*"

Phil laughed. The other two looked at him. He'd thought it was a joke. "Why?" he asked.

"Everything is man versus this and man versus that. It's so simple," Dan said, his voice rising. "It's man versus everything. It's me. It's you. It's us. It's in us. It's in—"

"Okay, okay, but it's a war story," Phil interrupted. "It should be *Man Versus Man.*"

"I'm the writer. I get to call it whatever I want. And it's *Man V. Nature.*" Dan crossed his arms, satisfied. He had made his point.

"Well, I'm calling it *Man Versus Man.* Try and stop me," Phil said. He meant it jovially, but joviality seemed to be dead, at least where he was concerned.

"I'd watch *Man V. Nature*," Ross said to Dan. His point was not lost on Phil.

"Oh, I would too," Phil chimed in so he'd feel included. He itched a spot on his ankle that he'd already scratched raw. Under his fingernails he smelled rot.

Dan slammed his fist down on the hot rubber side. "God, I wish I had a pen. Some paper, too." Then a look like happiness passed over his face. "When we're rescued, I'm going to sell that show and make you a star."

"Me?" Phil asked.

"No, not you."

Ross smirked. "You're the star of *Man Versus Man*, re-member?"

A flock of geese flew by their boat, their shit making splashes like tiny bombs in the water.

A kind of bare grief Phil saw in movies but rarely experienced himself bubbled up. He was not quick to trust it. He said, "Cool," agreeably.

Phil dipped his beer can into the lake and splashed it around to part the sun-warmed surface water so the icy stuff below could rise up. He let the can fill and drank it in one long gulp. "Why would I sleep with your wife? I had my own wife."

Dan and Ross chuckled and exchanged an incredulous look.

"Because your wife sucked, and my wife is awesome," Ross explained.

"Patricia didn't suck."

"Um, yes, she did. She sucked. And you hated her."

"No, I didn't. She hated me. But I loved her. I really did. That's the truth." He didn't know if that was the truth. Honestly, he probably didn't love her specifically, but he'd loved that she was a woman, acted like a woman, and had at one point, early on, seemed to love him. Or pretended to. But it didn't matter now. He hated her now.

Phil poured a can of water on his head. He filled it, did it again, and then again until Dan whined about water in the boat. Phil stumbled to kneel, pulled out his penis, and tried to aim over the side like they'd always done, but the

stream was weak and urine pooled in the lifeboat. Instead
of yelling, Ross and Dan shared a look, and again Phil was
at a loss for what it meant.

Dan pulled out a strip of jerky from a secret stash in his
shorts. He passed it to Ross, who held it up like evidence. It
wilted in the heat. To Phil, it smelled like real meat cooking
on a grill. Drool spilled down his chin.

"*This* is the last one," Ross said to Phil knowingly, and
pushed the length of it into his mouth.

o o o

Dan woke screaming "Fire!" and jumped up from the sag-
ging plastic bench. His shorts were wet, and a deep intesti-
nal smell wafted from him. Ross yanked down Dan's shorts
to reveal an oozing patch of holey flesh covering one entire
cheek. The smell forced a puke from Phil. Ross soaked his
T-shirt in lake water and gingerly pressed it to Dan's ass to
clean it. Dan stood naked like a toddler in the backyard sun.
A smile played at his lips as he surveyed the lake reaching
in all directions. He turned to Phil, who was rinsing out his
mouth. The boat shook, shivered.

"Does it look like it hurts?" he asked.

"It looks like it will kill you," Phil said.

Dan giggled. "It doesn't hurt one bit." He repeated it
under his breath, emphasizing each word, until the men
helped him lie on his side along the bottom of the boat.
There would be no more rotation of seats. Phil and Ross
settled next to each other for the foreseeable future.

Phil slept poorly, fighting off annoyed elbow jabs from
Ross. Phil wanted his sleep time to be an escape. He wanted

to dream of a girl, of Bren. But what if he called out her name and Ross heard? What about dreams of some vacation, some cabin in snowy woods, instead? A fireplace. Some beer. Or maybe he could dream of flying. Away. From here. In the end, he dreamed of birds, their talons puncturing his arms as they pried white worms from the blisters on his neck.

"Wake up," Dan hissed, slapping their thighs and feet, whatever was closest. He was frantic again. "Get your things together. We've got to go!"

Ross rubbed his eyes. "Where? Go where?"

Phil tried to get his bearings. He looked around. He touched his neck.

"Down there," Dan shrieked. He pointed into the water. "Listen, I've been hearing more about this war that broke out, you know, I told you about it." They nodded, bewildered. "Well, it's getting worse. Common citizens are taking up arms to push the rebels out, and it's full-on revolution all around us. You can hear it if you listen really hard." Dan squeezed his eyes in concentration. Phil heard a trickle of water, and saw Dan pee himself.

"It's a humanitarian nightmare. World War Three. The only safe place is under the surface. I mean, think about it." His eyes bulged. "It's kind of beautiful. This world collapses. But the world below this world—it flourishes. Man V. Nature. See?"

Dan propped his chin on the side of the boat and peered into the water. He marveled, "We are actually in the perfect position. Stuck out here, we are citizens of no world. And so we're totally welcome down there." Dan gazed at Phil with admiration. "I don't think I could have done it. But you have guts. You knew something was happening. You kept us out here. You're kind of a genius, man. I'm so dumb, I thought we were going to die. And soon." Dan laughed hard. "Turns out we're gonna live." He briefly air-guitared.

Phil blinked. Was he serious? "I didn't keep us here. I didn't know anything," he said cautiously.

Dan's chest heaved. He sweated. "Bren and the girls are already down there. Say hi, Ross," he said, waving at the water.

Ross's mouth gaped, but despite himself, he looked. "I don't see anything."

Dan clutched at his own shirt. "You're a terrible husband. Terrible father. You just broke their hearts. Right in two. Don't you see?" He twirled his finger in the water, creating ripples that moved farther away from him. He leaned out, peering closely at the center spiral he'd created.

Ross said, "Hey, pal, get yourself back into this boat."

Dan turned to Phil. "Don't you see?" he pleaded.

Phil shook his head.

Ross said again, "Get in here. You can't leave me. If you leave, I'll die of boredom."

Phil winced.

Dan choked out a real sob. "But I'm so tired, Ross." He said it like a secret he didn't want Phil to know.

Everything was still, and Phil thought maybe the moment had passed. Then quickly, easily, Dan slid his body over the side of the lifeboat. Phil managed to grab his foot, but the shoe slid off with a couple of kicks, and they watched Dan waggle and pull, like a kid diving for toys in a backyard pool, until the darkest water swallowed him.

"I've got to go in, get him," Ross said.

"We've got to get him," Phil corrected.

Neither man moved.

Air bubbles rose to the top for a few minutes and then the lake was calm.

"Fuck," Phil said, holding Dan's shoe in the air. Ross snatched it and threw it overhand, the force pitching the boat wildly. It plunked like a stone into the water. The ripples went on forever.

o o o

Phil thought Ross would make a play for the better seat, now that Dan was gone, but instead Ross slumped over, barely propped up by his own bones. Phil slid to the boat floor and stretched out. He stifled a groan of pleasure out of respect for Dan.

Ross didn't say anything all day. He just peered over the edge like he was looking for something important and kept almost seeing it.

When the sun began to set, Ross reached into a zippered pocket on the inside of his shorts.

"What's in there?" Phil craned his neck to see. Maybe it was food.

"It's nothing," Ross said, taking out an index card and a stubby pencil, the kind used at golf courses.

"You had paper and pencil this whole time? And you didn't give it to Dan?"

Ross waved the card in the air. "Too small to fit a whole TV show on, don't you think? Besides, I didn't remember I had it. What kind of asshole do you think I am? I would never do that to him." He bent over the card and began to scribble.

"What are you writing?"

"Nothing that concerns you. It's for my girls."

"Are you going to signal a bird to pick it up and fly it to them?"

Ross singsonged, "Meh. Meh. Meh. Meh. Meh," mocking Phil's comment, his whiny voice. He scooped water from the side of the lifeboat and flung it at Phil. Phil retaliated by filling his cupped hands and dousing Ross's lap and scorecard.

Ross leaped to his feet and the boat bottom folded, water rushing over the side. A cramp from sitting so long seized him and he lurched forward, bending deeply, so his face met Phil's. His sunburned eyeballs looked like the bottom of a dried lake bed. Tears burst from them and tracked through the grime on his face. "You expect me to believe you didn't do this on purpose?"

"Sit down! What are you talking about?"

"Strand us out here. You know, *run out of gas*."

Phil laughed. "Calm down."

"You just happened to forget to fill the tank? That's crap. We've been coming out here how many years?" Ross sat down with a thud, and more water poured in.

"That's baloney. You're crazy." True, Phil hadn't filled the tank up all the way. Dan and Ross hadn't offered him any money. It was weird. They usually did, but this time they'd just pretended to look at the map when he backed the boat trailer up to the pump. Gas was so expensive now. He'd felt uneasy ever since he'd picked up Ross. He and Dan, they'd been fine, talked about girls Dan could fix him up with now that he was single. But then Ross had gotten in the car. Phil thought then that maybe Bren had finally told Ross about the blow job. He'd always thought Ross acted weird around him, ever since. For years he'd assumed Ross knew. He wanted Ross to know, to know and to go on these trips with Phil anyway. Because they were such good friends and nothing could ruin that. And Phil could feel he'd gotten away with it. And then maybe it could happen again, with Bren. It had been a fantastic blow job. He'd been drunk, yes, but he still remembered it. She acted drunk, but he knew she wasn't. She had wanted to do it. And the fact that Bren never came to the door to see Ross off on these trips was proof to Phil. She was harboring some serious feelings for him. God, Bren. They used to have a ball together back in the day. They'd all go out when Phil visited for the holidays, him and Dan and Ross and Bren. Ross and Dan always drank too much and were a mess. But in basic training Phil learned how to act sober even when he wasn't, so he always offered to drive Bren home and then would rejoin Ross and Dan later. They never suspected anything. Bren was so giggly and her mouth was so big, with her sleek white teeth and that thin slippery tongue. They made out the first couple of visits, and he felt her up frantically. And when she was pregnant, her tits were unreal. And then, that fantastic blow job. But then she stopped going out with them when he was visiting. "She's with the kids," Ross would explain. And Phil always thought he saw a weird look on Ross's face.

"We weren't even going to come this year. Me and Dan," Ross said. "We talked. Yeah, we talked about stopping with this stupid week. We hate it. And Bren hates it when I go. Not because I leave her, but because of you. She says you're a creep. And she makes this face when she says it." Ross pruned his. "Me and Dan have our own week. In June. We go rock climbing. It's awesome. And we were planning even more weeks. Dan was seeing a girl. We were going to have them to the cabin. She's great. I bet you didn't even know about her. I bet you never even asked what was new with Dan. Like, 'Hey Dan, what's new with *you*?' " Ross looked like he might spit at Phil, head-butt him, but instead his face drooped pitifully. "But then you got divorced, and god, you were so fucked up. We felt bad because we're nice people. So we came, and now look. Dan is living with mermaids and it's World War Three, and we're never going to get out of this shitty, shitty rubber boat." He hung his head. "My girls." He wept.

Phil slumped against the hot, squeaky wall. He couldn't believe it. They felt sorry for him? Was that why they didn't give him any gas money? Because they didn't really want to be here? And Bren said he's a creep? He didn't believe it for a second. Did they really go rock climbing? Did they really have their own week?

As boys, when Phil asked to sleep over, Ross and Dan had told him their moms had said no. He'd had no reason to doubt it was true. Phil had done everything to make sure they were friends. He gave them candy, money, comic books. When they got older, he let them drink his parents' liquor and took the blame. He'd bribed his sister Maggie to have sex with Ross, who was still a virgin by the time he left for college. He didn't know she was a virgin too, but Ross told him. Ross said Maggie was a crybaby. Then Ross went off to college and met Bren. And Phil went into the army, developed a gambling habit, had a series of failed relationships, pined for Bren, finally settled for Patricia, quit gambling, thought his life would turn around. It had. He believed it had. Until a year ago, he believed that. And even though Ross and Dan hadn't wanted to come, in the end they came. That meant something, right?

"I'm sorry, boss. Please, I'll do anything," Phil said. He got goose bumps from the familiarity of wanting something he realized he couldn't have.

Ross's eyes were swollen and red, but hard. His mouth tightened into a smirk. "If you want to be my friend, you'll never talk to me again." He turned his head away and bent over his knees to sleep.

o o o

In the morning, Ross was gone. His water-warped golf scorecard was tucked into Phil's clenched hand. On it was written: *Got rescued! You looked so peaceful I decided not to wake you!*

All around Phil was the same still, gray water that had surrounded their boat for days. Weeks? Months? No land peeked out from behind the morning fog. No wake from a passing ship spread itself into thin ripples. Did Ross really get rescued?

Phil groaned an alone kind of groan: deep and howling, a major pitch-shifter. How many more signs did he need? Adrift on a lake for countless days without another soul in sight? No search parties? Friends who got rescued and left him behind, or who'd rather drown than stay in a boat with him? He'd rather drown than stay in a boat with himself. Life was over. He was tired of life. Life sucked. I want to live, he thought. Really live. Let go of the world. Wasn't there a way to get to the ocean from here? Everything is connected to an ocean somehow. Yeah, he could float up that seaway Dan mentioned, to the Arctic, where no lawyer could get to him. He could find a way to catch fish and just drift through icebergs and shower in whale spouts. Now, that was a life. Not like his. Divorced and forty. No kids. He should have taken that as a sign. She didn't want to have kids. What woman doesn't want to have kids? He kept waiting for her to say she wanted them. It's the guy who's supposed to not want kids; the wife is supposed to be like, "We're having kids, you asshole," until the guy feels pushed into it and resentful. But when they pop out he's supposed to realize that his kids are the reason life makes sense, and then he's supposed to love his wife even more, want to get a better job, discover his new life purpose as protector of his family. That's how it's supposed to go. Except she didn't want kids. Didn't even want to talk about it.

Phil wept. The crust around his eyes melted back to goo. He wept for all the kids he never had. He'd always wanted kids, ever since he was a kid. Since going fishing with his dad down at Pickerel Lake, standing on the shore, casting off. The silence. The stillness. The heat penetrating their baseball caps. Here comes his sister, fast, yelling down the path, and here's his dad hushing her and then, seeing her little shamed face, picking her up and swinging her upside down over the water until she wails, then cradling her in his arms until she laughs. It made so much sense even back then. That's what you do. You have a bunch of them and they're your friends. They look like you. You give them your feelings. It's animal. It's basic. What kind of cunt doesn't want kids? "Stretch marks," she had said once, laughing it off. His whole life. Wasted.

Phil's grief pulled him to the bottom of the lifeboat and he curled up. The water there, trapped and warm, pruned him.

The golf pencil wavered by his head. He plucked it and drew a stick figure on the other side of the scorecard, in a small corner that hadn't already been written on and scratched over by Ross. He made out *I love you* but could read no more of Ross's words.

From the figure, Phil drew a thought bubble. *Hello*, he wrote within its girlish borders.

At first the stick figure was Patricia, but he was silenced by the desire to say the perfect thing to either hurt her or to fix things. Then it was Ross, but he could only think of apologies, and for what, he couldn't say. He missed his friend. Was the figure a child? He couldn't see it; it was unfamiliar. A stick figure. It didn't look like him at all. He stared at his companion mutely. Eventually the paper fell from his fingertips and disintegrated in the rank stew where he lay, fetal.

He roused himself in time for a puke over the side, and in the bile-soured water he saw his own reflection. Who will miss me? he asked himself. No one had. It was real, a fact. The proof—his solitude. He stared, seemed to wait days for the answer. He laid his head down, smelled the hot rubber.

At the next daybreak Phil took notice of, he lifted his head to a new smell. Pine. The morning fog rolled away like a stage curtain to reveal rocky cliffs, evergreened at the top, on either side of him, as the large lake funneled into an ever-narrowing channel. He saw the current quicken around his boat, swirling, tugging, caressing.

He thought of Canada. Of the war. Of beluga whales, their pinked heads breaking through the black surface to breathe, misting everything into a watercolor.

"Don't shoot," he yelled to all the hiding rebels. He held up his hands in mock horror, his voice echoing off the bluffs surrounding him, and it sounded as though the hills were full of men begging for the same mercy as he was. He doubled over and laughed until he wheezed like the aged.

The water flattened, and Phil saw the hull of a ship maneuver a bend, miles in the distance.

The current carried him toward the enormous vessel, a tanker of some sort. When finally next to it, he rapped his knuckles on the side. It was metal, and the rumble it threw back was like dungeon doors closing. Water had worn away the blue paint, which now only covered the higher-up walls. He sliced his palm against the large white barnacles stuck to the hull, and blood the color of cartoon apples flowed out.

A real boat.

Just then a rope ladder unfurled down the side, and Phil grabbed hold.

MARRYING UP

Just before the world got bad, I married for love, a man who was funny and brilliant, but small. He could not pick me up the way I'd watched the men do to women on television. I'd never been twirled as I laughed, my head back, my leg in a kick, all to some lighthearted song. But no matter. I loved him. I rested my chin on the top of his head when I was tired, and when he was, I wrapped my stronger arms around his small body. We were happy.

Then one day I became feverish and was unable to leave our bed, and so he ventured out to find medicine at the pharmacy. He said, "Be right back, my love," grabbed an umbrella, and left. I'm told that even though he swung the umbrella wildly, he was set upon before he'd even left the front stoop of the building.

My next lover was funny but not as bright. He was much taller, however, and with a little more muscle that showed beneath his flesh, though sometimes it just made him seem hungry rather than strong. I'd seen him in the building; he fixed things. I asked him to fix my leaky faucet, and then I asked him to stay.

He could twirl me, but once when I kicked my leg his back gave and we tumbled to the floor. I brought hot pads to place under him and made a bed for us where he had fallen so he wouldn't have to move. He told me jokes as we lay there, and he laughed, then grimaced, each time forgetting that it hurt him to laugh. But I liked that about him. We planned to marry.

One night, very late, the door buzzer woke us. He sat up and stepped into his slippers.

I said, "Don't go out there."

He said, "But someone's at the door."

The buzzer rang again. It's the kind of shrill buzzer found in old cities full of angry people. The kind that always catches you off guard.

I said, "Don't go," and I grabbed his arm.

He shook me free. "What if someone needs help?" Did I mention he was also a very good-hearted man? He was.

"No one needs help," I said, feeling like an awful person. "It's a trap."

He looked at me like he didn't know who I had become. I was so ashamed I couldn't look back, even though I knew I was right. I'd heard the stories. I knew better than to answer the door.

"Someone needs help," he said resolutely, shrugging on his robe. I'm told he fought hard, scrappily, but was dragged to his knees, then dragged down the street. For days afterward bits of his torn pajamas blew around, up in the air, into the naked trees. I watched them through my window.

Soon a new man moved into the apartment above me. His footsteps rattled my lamps and china, shook plaster dust down onto my dinner. I knew the kind of power behind footsteps like that. And eventually I married him.

He terrified me. He was more than twice my size. Making love felt like getting run over. I was pancaked like in cartoons. My ribs crunched if he was on top, and my hips were belted with bruises if he was behind. He twirled me until I puked.

He wasn't particularly bright, but he wasn't stupid. He wasn't funny. When I cracked a joke, he just stared. He was violent.

But he took me to the park. It seemed like forever since I'd been outside, but we could go to the pond and feed the remaining ducks, the ones too diseased to consume, and my husband felled all those who set upon us like they were tiny saplings. It felt like a small miracle to be able to go outside.

o o o

Each day, my husband left the house swinging a baseball bat. When it splintered, he used his fists. By the end of the day, our street was littered with bodies. At night I dressed his knuckles with ointment, wrapped them in bandages, and did it again the following night, and the night after. Each morning, the tenuous scabs ripped open; the wounds had no time to heal.

When I went into labor, he carried me outside, and we were set upon. My hair was pulled. Someone punched my round belly. But this was a momentary scourge. My husband drove through the wall of them like we were all on a football field and I was the odd-shaped ball in his arms.

All around us were moans, hands grabbing as we ran. I thought, How can I bring a child into this world? Then I thought, At least our child will have half my husband's genes. Whatever the world brings, surely the child of a man like this can meet it.

I almost didn't make it through the delivery, the child was so large. Its aggressive squirming tore things in me. I was put under.

o o o

I was weak from the delivery, and now my boy took every last nutrient; he sucked me dry. I was too exhausted after nursing to move. He grew to an enormous size, a size that scared me, but also delighted me. I was desperate for him to be so big and strong that nothing could ever harm him.

By the time he was six months old, he was too big for me to lift. But he was hungry all the time. To nurse, my husband placed the child on my chest while I lay still beneath. He had to stay home to lay and lift the child off me all day. Eventually he lost his job.

"I think you should stop nursing," he said one night.

I lay beneath our boy, flattened, barely breathing from the weight of him.

"But how will he grow?"

"Look at you." He squeezed my flaccid bicep. I tried to make a muscle, but the arm just trembled. "I doubt you're giving him the kind of nutrition he needs."

We switched to nutrient packs that he bought from the corner market.

We were a sight. I was all bones; my husband was

bruised and bloodied from his nutrient pack outings. Our boy, though, was magnificent; he stomped around the house, able to reach things on the highest shelf for me. His shoulders were broad like a draft animal's, and he carried me around on them like I weighed zero. He teetered on his trunkish legs like a toddler because he was one. It was scary and thrilling to wobble up so high. I traced the filigree patterns on the ceiling of our once fine home.

o o o

My husband insisted we all eat the nutrient packs for strength. We needed it. A man on a lower floor had been attacked in his apartment. We couldn't count on staying home to keep us safe. But the nutrient packs had the opposite effect on me. I grew heavy but not strong; my muscles quivered under the extra weight.

My husband insisted we run sprints across our living room. Three times a day we did circuits. After lunch, we bench-pressed. He spotted me on the bench, but mostly he lifted the bar for me, and shamed me while I blubbered. Our son watched us with curiosity.

By twenty months he could bench almost as much as his father. He no longer wore clothes; nothing fit. We wrapped him in bath towels instead of diapers. He stomped around and soaked through them onto all the furniture. I did load upon load of laundry. Nothing smelled right in our house any longer.

For money and goods, my husband ran errands for the other apartment owners in our building. He went to the market for them. He acted as a guard when they had to go outside. He escorted them if they had to go to work. Our apartment became stocked with supplies and strange luxuries, all bartered for my husband's services. Fine sheets, china cups, silver trays. I hammered those silver trays onto one wall so my boy could watch himself do push-ups and bicep curls across their reflective surfaces.

o o o

One night, my husband came home with his shirt torn, his abdomen gashed with thick bloody lines like from the tines of a garden fork.

"It's getting much worse," he huffed. He made me do extra sets of jumping jacks and squats and then squeezed all my major muscle groups while I tensed. I wanted this to lead him to make his violent kind of love to me, but he just went to the table and put his head down.

I checked the door and turned all the extra bolts. Sometimes my husband locked just two, like it was some test of fate. Could he ward off the intruders with brute strength if they got through a measly two locks? Three? We all knew he could, but I liked eight, a nice curvy number that had a lot in common with infinity. At least in looks. I bolted eight.

Our boy carried me to his room, and I read him a book while he tried to do crunches like his dad.

"You want to feel it deep in your belly," I instructed. I knelt beside him as he struggled and failed and placed my palm right below his navel. I pressed down, and his breath pushed out and I felt the contraction while his head and shoulders lifted like they were tethered to the ceiling.

o o o

My husband made plans to move us to another city, one that was reportedly safer. He said, "We can't raise our son here. I thought we could, but we can't."

"Going elsewhere is much more difficult than staying put," I argued.

"It's one thing for us to be cooped up here. But he needs to be able to go outside. To grow."

He looked at our boy and nodded, and our boy nodded back, but he was only mimicking his father; he didn't understand what was happening. He lay on the crashed-down couch, broken long ago by his weight and his father's, and sucked down a nutrient pack. He appeared to grow in chest circumference right before my eyes.

"He's fine," I said.

But my husband had made up his mind. He sighed and looked me up and down. "I'll protect you as much as I can," he said. "We both will." Then he looked at his hands, swallowing the inherent *but*.

I went to the window. Of course I knew what he meant, and I was angry. I had been strong once. I had made it this far. Now, because I'd given him a child, a son, I was weak and would be left behind.

I thought about how I might fare here alone. I looked through the lattice of the window gate at the smoke from the many fires that licked the sky. As the sun fell for the night, it glowed a sickly purple, like it had an awful flu and was giving up.

I could maybe last a week or two. If they noticed that my husband no longer patrolled the street, they might investigate the apartment, find me here, and have a field day. I looked at my son. I wondered if he would fuss at having to say good-bye. How would he remember me? I'd be that funny woman who used to ride on his shoulders. He might remember the feel of me there, almost weightless in light of his strength. But what more could he remember? That I taught him crunches? Gave him all my fortitude? Even though he looked like a man at times, he was just a baby still. It was strange to know, looking at them, that they would make it and be fine. And stranger to know that they looked at me and knew I would not. And that we would go anyway.

My husband unfolded maps at the table. He traced routes with his giant fingertip.

"We have to cross the mountains. The people there are wild," he warned, his tone defeated.

But I felt buoyed by the idea. Mountains are beautiful. It must be springtime, I thought, and maybe there would be flowers. Maybe we would dip in a mountain lake, blue like my boy's eyes, cold enough to pucker my skin. We might hear birds calling rather than people hollering. If we went for a hike, were we as likely to be set upon as we were when we left this building? I found it hard to believe that anything could be as brutal as our neighbors.

I remembered seeing pictures of people living in the bottoms of large trees. They were old pictures, even back in my childhood, but surely it was still done. I'd seen whole cars being driven through big hollowed trunks as a stunt. "Maybe we could live in a tree," I dreamed.

My husband said angrily, "Don't be a fool. The mountains are dangerous. They're not like the cities. The city is still civilized."

I laughed, even though he'd said it straight-faced.

I took his damaged hands in mine. With his arms slack and heavy, I could barely lift them to my lips. In another time, I thought, I wouldn't have given him a second glance walking down the street. He's outlandish, his body triangular. But maybe he was a good man, and I wondered, under different circumstances or given more time, if he might surprise me. We might surprise each other. And isn't that really what makes for a nice life with someone?

"You told a joke," I said proudly.

He said sadly, "Ha."

We made love that night, and it was almost tender. Like he felt bad and wanted to remember me in some soft-lit way. So I pulled at his hair and I scratched away the bandages on his hands, bit open the scabs until they bled. His eyes watered, but he took it. I was trying to show him. Don't give up on me yet.

Finally, he batted me away like a pest. My eye swelled shut, a tinny ring expanded in my ear. He turned from me and sulked.

With my good eye I looked toward my son's room, where he slept, peaceful and trusting. I had made it this far. I slipped quietly from the bed. I could be brutal too, even in the safety of our once fine home.

IT'S COMING

The alarm goes off smack in the middle of the presentation. We try to look at each other in the darkened office, in the dim glow of PowerPoint colors; we scoff, we are stunned. Someone says, "This is a drill, right?" We look to the head of the table, where our boss usually sits, but he is not here today; another meeting, another city. Of course Roger usurps our missing boss's authority. "Yes," he says in a deeper than natural voice, "just a drill, people," and we are forced to continue absorbing the presentation.

But soon we're whispering under the drone of the presenter. Someone says, "I mean, what are the odds it chose *our* building, right?" Someone replies, "Well, it *is* the tallest." Someone counters, "No, it's not." There is some whispering back and forth on this point.

At the other end of the table, someone hisses, "I always thought it would come at night, while we slept."

"Yeah," someone agrees, "what could be more terrible than taking out a whole subdivision of vulnerable sleeping families?"

"I *know*! I feel so much safer when I come through these doors in the morning."

"Yes, it *must* be a drill." Suddenly these two are holding hands and trembling.

The presenter finally stops the PowerPoint because someone is crying loudly, "It's not a drill, it's not a drill," and we all kind of know the crier is right.

Then we're moving quickly, snapping, *This is it, people.* We remind one another of protocol as we gather our belongings. *Be professional. Focus. Just grab the essentials. You won't care about your stupid umbrella when it's got you by the legs.* Executive chairs swirl as we pull sweaters, purses, suit coats, from their backs and pour from the boardroom.

The emergency exit is just squeezing shut; the whole floor has already evacuated, the last of them leaving an overwhelming whiff of some childish perfume. We hear the thudding stampede down the cement stairs, and we are about to follow, fling that emergency door wide again, when we hear panicked screams coming from far down the stairwell. The screams become terrible, wet and pulpy, and the stampede of feet reverses back up the stairs, though it sounds greatly diminished.

We run away from the door and pass a conference room where new hires have been ensconced in a training meeting. They huddle under the long oval table. They don't know the office emergency protocol yet. It's on page 140 of their manual, and there's no way they got that far this morning. Thompson, who had been leading the meeting, is quaking under the head of the table. No doubt he hadn't thoroughly prepped for the training session and hadn't reread protocol;

he's a winger, not a preparer, which is sometimes advanta-
geous and other times unfortunate. Currently, it is unfortunate; the conference room has been left leaderless. We shrug
as we run by, as if to say *Oops* and *Good luck* and *Don't
follow us.*

Past the conference room, we whisper *Parachutes* extra
quietly so the new hires won't hear. We run to our win-
dowed offices, where our emergency parachutes are locked
in safes. They're a secret executive perk. But the parachutes
are gone. The only people who knew about them were the
secretaries who ordered them, ordered the safes, hid them,
and told us our combinations. It appears they have also
taken them. And there they go. The glossy white canopies
float past our windows, our secretaries' skirts blown up
over their faces. And we thought they could be trusted.

Now we want to panic, but we calmly huddle instead.
What now? we ask ourselves. "This way," someone yells,
pointing to the other hallway. We run.

At the end of the hallway we have two options: go right,
down the hall that leads to the break room; go left, down
the hall to where the bathrooms are. With so many of us we
are funneling and tight and someone yells "Split up!" and
that seems smart, so we split and some of us go to the break
room and some of us go to the bathroom.

In front of the men's and women's we hesitate; we are
a mix of men and women. Should we continue to split, or
break company policy and enter a bathroom that does not
correspond to our sex? No one does that, not even during
holiday parties when drunk. It is one of the very followed
rules. But if we split, we worry we'd feel vulnerable. If it

brutalized the women who hid alone in the women's, we'd feel horrible. We'd feel equally bad if it brutalized the men in the men's. It would be much better if everyone had stayed together and gone to the left; there would be a larger number of men and women and we wouldn't have to be so worried.

But in the break room there are problems, too. Too many of us went right. We yelled, *This is too many!* as we squeezed down the hall, but no one wanted to be the one to turn the other way, cross that open vulnerable T-space again; what if it was bounding down right at that very moment and caught us in its grotesque arms? In the break room we cram in, jostle for positions away from the door, but there are only so many of those positions, and some of us can't even get in the room and we're left squirming in the doorway. We admit our mistake because it is always best to. *This won't work!* we scream.

Meanwhile, outside the restrooms someone is yelling, "It won't think to look in the women's." Why? Who knows, but we all agree with the logic and tumble in.

We can't believe how nice the women's bathroom is. It smells good; it is so clean. We huddle close, away from the door, pushing into the handicap stall. In bursts the break room crew, insisting it wouldn't work. It's good to be together again. Until Gloria starts whisper-whining that she wished she'd stayed in the break room so she could eat her lunch. "I brought leftover noodles. I was looking forward to them." We listen, but we can't imagine how she can feel hungry at a time like this. Then she gets weepy. "They were from my date last night. It went really well. You know how hard it's been for me." We know. We nod. "I really liked him. I was going to think about him while I ate the noodles." She bawls. A few of us succeed in shushing her into a light simper. We think about Gloria's date, what he might have looked like, what kind of noodles they'd been, if the date had gone as well as she claims, because Gloria is known to embellish. We think about our own lunches and why they don't contain something through which to experience one last joy, if in fact we've reached our end. We think about our loved ones, if we have any. We press in close. We listen for it.

Stan is right next to Susan, his eyes fixed on the floor, jimmying his hand in his pocket. Quickly we realize that he can see up Susan's skirt in the high polish of the marble floors, can see her soft thigh meet her floral panties, and that he is incrementally stiffening; Susan realizes it too.

Stan senses a heightening of the already heightened stillness of the lavatory and understands he's been discovered. He looks up sheepishly, his jiggling slows; he removes his hand from his pocket and blushes behind his large glasses.

We're about to groan, *Stan*, as in, *That's really unprofessional*, but Susan looks around at us, like she has had one of our industry's sought-after *aha* moments, and then she grabs Stan's hand and pushes it up her skirt, and after the briefest surprised pause he finger-fucks her right there in front of us until her thighs glisten and we have to cover her mouth so her orgasm won't give us away. Of course, she bites us wildly, leaves our fingers hurt and wet. And Stan, wearing the most tremendous grin, his glasses all askew, conjures a pulsing, rounded erection that eventually gives way beneath his soft twill pants, darkening a spot like drool on a pillowcase, just from bringing Susan to climax in the women's bathroom on what might very well be the last day of our lives. We watch with acute envy, but we can't exactly do it ourselves, now can we?

As Susan collapses into Stan's arms, panting and mewing, we hear the muffled sounds of limbs snapping, bodies being cleaved, each hiccupping death caw; the new hires have been found. "Let's roll," someone says, and we abandon the bathroom.

Layered bodies block the emergency exit stairwell. Bloodied viscera slides under the door into the hall from the conference room. Inside it sounds like forty tigers wrestling. We have to think. We know what our best move is, but we don't want to admit it. We exchange looks; the burdened looks of having to make the tough decisions. They are familiar to us; we are executives. We are about to say, *Our only way out is up*, when we hear a man and woman giggling from just left of the center of our huddle.

Stan has yanked Susan's blouse open, the buttons splaying from the torn threads. Her large purple nipple creases between his fingertips. And she's started up her moaning again. *Come on, you guys*, we hiss, as in, *That's really unprofessional*. But there they are. Now Stan's shoes are off and his pants down, and he has surprisingly hard ropy legs atop which sits his marshmallow torso. Susan fondles his bobbing prick; it seems to nod yes. She is all the way nude, and her breasts fall much lower than we noticed before; they are not just big, which we'd known, but heavy, and her stomach protrudes enough that they seem to rest on it. And it isn't that it isn't attractive; it is just, again, surprising. And we marvel at how bodies never look naked the way they look in clothes. *When will we learn?* we chide ourselves, and wish we'd spent more time admiring one another, our loved ones, ourselves.

From the conference room it sounds like forty alligators wrestling in a swamp, and tides of blood pulse out from under the door.

Stan and Susan clatter to the floor, their limbs jutting and tied together; our huddle is greatly disturbed.

"Leave them," someone shouts. And we run.

Because this is our building, we know there is a short stairwell that continues above the regular stairwell—the one filled with bodies—beyond the Do Not Enter door. It has an unfinished quality, though it is safe. If anyone takes anyone anywhere during a holiday party, it is probably here, and it is probably low-level clerks, lonely new hires, our deceitful secretaries; they fumble past forgotten panels of drywall and unused rods of pipe to find a railing to get bent over, a wall to leverage against.

We clamber and slip over the flayed bodies blocking the door; the inside of their skin is slick, and sheets of their raw, violet muscle seem to spasm. We hope it is a trick of the wavering light. All the way down the stairwell is a thick corpse wall. Just as we'd expected. There would be no way to push through so many mangled parts of former employees.

Up we go.

Flickering work spotlights dangle here and there, smelling like the overtired motors of electronics; the stairwell is treacherous in a pall of brown light. We grope our way along the walls and rails. Up higher, lights blaze everywhere, and we have to shield our eyes. Workmen must have abandoned some project at the first sound of the alarms. Perhaps their bodies are part of the corpse wall.

And here we are.

We hear, "Wait," and below appear Stan and Susan. They trail naked, and we can hear it bounding close behind them. Stan's scared little prick flops between his legs and Susan's breasts clap together with each panicked stride. They are holding hands, fingers entwined and intimate, like they've spent a lifetime strolling along, holding one another. And that's real terror we see in their eyes, because they aren't concerned just for their own survival but for each other's. Their feet are bloodied, and they struggle, slip, tug each other along, they try to kiss and hug, and they cry and cry.

It follows their scent.

And oh, we can't tell you what we see next, it's just too horrible. And sad. But it buys us some time to get out to the roof.

When we heave the roof door we scatter a thousand pigeons who thought they'd found a good hiding spot. Think again, pigeons. We stack roof debris in front of the door to slow its advance.

The alarm wails over the whole city. From the roof edge we see people flooding into the streets, down the streets and onto the wide boulevards, along the boulevards and then out to the multilane highways, where vehicles stall in the scrum and drivers abandon them to join the swift-footed exodus; they spiral around exchanges that spill out to the state highways until those highways narrow into county roads through small towns and then vein into neighborhood lanes and dissolve into fields of hay; all those people fan out across that dead autumn yellow until they reach the woods, and then we can track their movement by the quivering of the treetops as the millions jostle those poor trunks and trammel the forest floor. It is like a great green rolling swell that will deliver them to the actual ocean's edge, and we wonder what will happen then. Will they wade out in confusion? Or will they buck momentum, backpedal, scatter throughout the forests and mountains, decide speciously that they have a natural aptitude for survival-by-hiding-spot? We would have loved to know; and we could have: it's a tall building, some say the tallest, and from here we can see everything. But just then the alarm quiets; the city has emptied save for us. And we notice a rhythmic rumbling under our shined shoes. It is finished with Stan and Susan, and it's coming for us.

We vow to one another not to let it get us alive; that we won't cower in fear and be taken; we fought this long. We will jump when it forces the roof door open. We will jump together on the count of three. We are executives, dammit, and this is our building, our company. The carnage in the hallways and stairwells is our carnage; those were our employees.

We stand wind-shocked at the building lip. The sun shrinks behind grim clouds. "I will look it right in the eye," someone resolves weepily. We grit our teeth.

The door cracks ever so slightly, slowly, as though it relishes these final moments. Our protective stack of garbage tumbles. "Remember, on three," someone chokes.

Then Roger says, "Wait. Here's an idea." He steps off

the ledge and faces us. "Imagine." He holds his hands out like he's positioning a portrait; a portrait of his idea.

We're trembling. We're wetting ourselves. But we're listening.

"Ask yourselves this: Does it really want to kill us?"

Harsh orange light from the stairwell seeps into the gray sky as the door opens more. It seems to be there, just behind shadow, gathering itself.

Did you see the stairwell?

The new hires are just fluid now.

Roger puts a hand up to quiet us. "I know, I know. But we're top tier. Up here." He plateaus a hand above his own head. "We're executives."

So were Stan and Susan.

Roger shakes his head. "They lost focus. They lacked leadership. Now look at them," he says. "Trust me. We've got something it can use. We're golden." Then he humbly scrunches his shoulders as if to say, *But what do I know?* which is pure Roger, because he can clearly hear the murmur of dissent he has sparked. He rocks back and forth on his wing tips, smiling. Roger loves mixing it up.

Someone starts the count.

"One."

We clasp hands. Some of us squeeze our eyes shut.

"Wait, let's think about what Roger said," a voice pleads.

It's quiet up here on the roof above a city with no people. The only sounds now are its harsh breath behind the splitting door; the creaking of city buildings that, lightened of their human loads, now sway easily in the wind; and Roger, whistling.

We hear someone say "Two."

Now, hold on.

We want to be sure.

Blood-slick talons curl around the door. But thanks to Roger, some of us can only see them as friendly talons, potential-business-partner talons. Our hearts bassoon in our ears. There is movement on the ledge. Some fingers are panicking out of the hands they're holding, while others are scratching to hold on. Our exhales are ponderous; they churn the wind. Down the line, negotiations begin. Will some latent instinct kick in before our bodies meet concrete? That is our hope; but there is no guarantee. And if we survive the jump, will life in this new world be worth living? Hard to say; we'd need some polling done. Will we be one last flesh dinner for it if we stay? There is always that risk. Is Roger right? "I'm right," says Roger. Then what should our course of action be?

Well?

It's coming.

Let me think.

We surprise ourselves by wishing Stan and Susan were still here. Roger claims they lacked leadership, but they went with their guts. They took risks. They yearned and they followed through. *They ate the noodles*, we realize, and are pleased with our metaphor. Sure, they came to a terrible end, but under all that blood and those tears, we swear we saw a peace like nothing we've ever known. We would have loved to feel that kind of peace. But look, now the door has opened, and it's coming fast.

METEOROLOGIST
DAVE SANTANA

More than once when watching Dave Santana give the local weather report, Janet put her hands in her pants. On the day he introduced the new weather screen—over which he smoothed his hands, bringing clouds in from the west or heavy rains south instead of moving Velcro-backed pictures of happy suns or mischievous-looking puffy clouds—Janet imagined *she* was the weather screen as she bounced astride the arm of her sofa.

But during the winter's first nor'easter, Dave Santana was on the air five whole days, in hourly updates and long talk spots during the regular news. And Janet's slender vibrator waited in her robe pocket or under the band of her underpants: at the ready, both necessary and a privilege, like a limb.

He'd carried them through the storm. From the first weather watch, through preparations, to the storm itself and its sad aftermath. Sad because people lost their homes, some even their lives, but Janet thought Dave looked sad because it had to end. As if he was thinking, as he recapped those tragic days, about getting into his car and going back to the condo he'd bought with his meteorologist's paycheck, which was big enough to support a family though he was a bachelor, and making some macaroni and cheese and watching reruns until he fell asleep. A moment of greatness he'd commanded was over through no fault of his own. She could relate. She tried to guide her students; she was a paragon in the area where their mothers had failed them—how to really have it all. But she could only teach them so much. When a few of them inevitably got pregnant by senior year, it felt like a personal blow. This disappointment that she and Dave shared—this synchronicity—aroused her.

Though he was classically unattractive—short and balding, his light-colored skin and hair hardly distinguishable from one another, and his eyebrows almost nonexistent—he *was* a New Englander. She appreciated the spirit of men from the Northeast. They didn't have the dreaminess of men from the Plains, where the sky was so big they got lost in it; or the lethargy of men from the Northwest, whose brains were rotted by rain; or the Southwest, where men strove to be coarse and dry. She'd been with them all. Men from the Northeast were practical, they could handle anything because they lived through the worst winters, hottest summers, and most beautiful falls. New England men bore all things. There was nothing quite as exciting to her as when Meteorologist Dave Santana let the word *nor'easter* roll out of his mouth, all juicy with meaning and menace, like a slick tongue. Plus, he was her neighbor.

With the storm pushed out, the winds flattened, and the skies no longer in need of interpretation, Janet waited for him to return to his town house, so torturously close. She hoped he'd still be bearing the disappointment that any end brings. She knew she could make him feel better.

o o o

When Dave Santana arrived, Janet slipped into her robe and opened her front door to icy air; she watched him gather his things from his blue compact and cleared her throat.

Dave startled. Then an expression settled on his face when he saw her—one she would have liked to think was mild pleasure, but she knew better; it was a mild something else. She had been to the door many times in the past year, inviting him in for drinks, to change a lightbulb, to kill a field mouse. Mostly, she tried to force herself upon him and each time was rebuked. "Janet, I'm tired," or "I have to wake early for the fisherman's forecast." Once he grabbed her wrists angrily, saying, "I'm a *meteorologist*," as if that alone should explain some principle to her. Was it that he was too good or too lowly for her? But the last time, after liquor was plied, something more happened. A fondle, a kiss, timid at first, then lingering, as if Dave Santana was deciding something. Then he scrunched his face and left. For weeks after, she stopped trying, told herself she wasn't that pathetic, and romped with some easies from a bar she liked in the next town. But this nor'easter and Dave's commanding presence on her television night after night after night broke her. She yanked the neck of her robe so it was loose and low.

"Janet," he said. "It's a little cold for slippers."

"Don't worry about me—I'm always hot," she said,

sliding her hand up the door and easing her hip out. No change, not even a twitch of his lips. "Listen, I'm dying to ask you about those wind gusts we had. Just how fast are we talking?" she asked in her best fascinated voice. With *wind gusts*, she saw a slight smile.

"And just how scared should I still be? Because you know how scared I get," she said. She let the robe slip off one shoulder, then drew it back up and shivered so her hips shimmied. She wanted him to note how vulnerable she could make herself. Then he could decide to protect her or fuck her. Protection was fine, fucking better, but both was best.

"Janet," he repeated, but his edge softened. "I know how scared you get." He came inside, saying, "But the weather is nothing to be scared of. Even storms like this." He accepted her gin. She had high hopes.

After dropping a coaster and bending toward him to pick it up, her robe opening slightly, she felt him relax. She knew he had looked, heard his voice catch in his throat as he explained how he measured wind speed. When she reached across him to retrieve a magazine for that article on Atlantic currents she'd saved for a moment like this, he subtly copped a feel. Finally, with a deep breath, knowing this would be the end of the evening or the beginning, she went for it; she slipped her hand between his legs during an extended lesson on atmospheric pressure—*Air has weight, like a person, weight that is pushing against us all the time, even now*—and after a look of surprise, he tore open her robe. He scanned all of her like a scientist. She reclined, traced a finger down herself and watched his eyes follow to where it disappeared. She thought she saw that slight smile play again. Then he flipped his belt open, slunk from his khakis, and fell upon her. They bumped to the floor, pushed the coffee table away, their limbs a puzzle until he flung her legs wide and fit himself in.

She didn't need to act; it was good. But still she did everything a little louder, breathier, rougher, just to be sure he got the message: *You are important to me. Even after the storm, I need you.*

They continued in the bedroom. And when he finally slept, she smoothed down his chest and back hair. "So passionate," she murmured.

In the morning, she watched him sneak out. He closed the bedroom door gently, but by the time he reached the front door his mind was elsewhere and he let it slam. If she'd been asleep, it would have jolted her awake; she'd be disoriented, wondering what had happened. But instead she anticipated it, felt the soft tremble through her body.

o o o

Janet tried to run into Dave again, somehow get him over to her place. But he never answered when she knocked. Didn't respond to the notes she taped to the door or his car windshield. Sometimes she glimpsed his back as he entered his house, or his shoe as he got in his car, his face obscured by morning glare upon the windows. It began to feel as if he'd never existed. Except when she watched him nightly she remembered his weight pushing against her.

One morning, Janet noticed a woman leaving Dave's town house. Then on several more mornings after that she saw her again. The woman was mousy; her limp brown hair hung straight down her back unless she had it pulled up in a thin, messy ponytail. She always left early, clearly needing to return to her own home to get ready for work. They were not serious enough for her to keep her things at his house, Janet decided.

o o o

And then it was spring.

Janet won another teaching award: Teacher of the Year, five years running. It was like a perfect school-year farewell from the girls, who adored her. It's never a landslide, but the girls outnumber the boys, and, well, the girls love me, she'd say when her fellow teachers unenthusiastically congratulated her. The teachers all disliked her, she was certain. In their opinion Janet was scary. That was their word for people who were better than them. At everything. And always had been. She'd stopped playing humble years ago, and because of it adults avoided her. They didn't know how to be around someone with no secret shame, guilt, trauma, or self-hatred.

Meanwhile, the teen girls experienced awe. They didn't know yet to be afraid of people like Janet. They looked at her and thought, Beauty! Brains! Confidence! Now here's something I can aspire to. They were one step away from adulthood and needed that extra push, and Janet was happy to give it to them, to keep them smart and out of trouble. She'd even designed special after-school sex-ed classes just for girls, and they were grateful. If it meant a lesson in the perfect blow job so sex was unnecessary, or inventive ways to put on a condom so it seemed like a treat to wear one?

She knew several tricks. Tips on how to be the seducer so as to control the proceedings? Seductress was her middle name. Be the parent signing off on birth control? Why not? She felt they were all her daughters.

The men in her life said she was too bossy in bed, always repositioning them and sighing when they did things wrong—There. No. *There.* But really, how hard is it to please a woman? Had they ever even tried? Even *she* had tried. Certainly it wasn't always easy. And so many women were so needy, then overly grateful. Especially the mothers. Like Mrs. Howard from parent-teacher conferences. Those aching eyes. Janet had thought, Why not? It had to have been this woman's first orgasm—or first good one. After, she curled into Janet's body and cooed until Janet finally said, as kindly as she could—she wasn't cruel exactly— "Enough," and began to dress. The look on Mrs. Howard's face: like she'd seen a ghost, maybe two. Janet avoided her calls after. There were only a few.

One man, some years ago, she'd been very optimistic about. He was a teacher; smart, sexy in a blazer, no tie; his shirt was always unbuttoned an extra button to display a manly spray of hair. He didn't mind her in bed; he was responsive. He pepped up when she boxed his ears with her legs and yelled, "Faster!" He got harder when she insisted, "Deeper," and he said, "Yes, Janet," as if he were saying, "Yes, ma'am." And he could do it too, huffing and groaning as though summiting a mountain while he pumped: his forearms and biceps tight from the strain of pulling her hips higher and toward him. A wild fear would rise in her that he could break through whatever barrier existed between them

and lose himself in the mess of her intestines. It was the best
sex she'd had up to that point. But soon he began to reveal
his disappointment in life. He'd always thought he'd be in
politics, attending dinners with the president or accepting
senatorial bribes. He never imagined he'd be a teacher in a
small city that wasn't even coastal, though it was close. He
got glum and expected comfort, for her to say he was special, could do anything—whatever women were supposed
to say to men who'd been told to expect big things from life.
They usually never considered that *big* could simply mean a
stable job, mostly happiness, occasional good-to-great sex.
She'd never been told to expect anything, and so she just did
what she wanted and told her students to do the same. She'd
won her teaching awards because she did what she loved
and did it well, not because she expected to be rewarded.
Dave Santana was important not because he thought he
should be but because he did important work, and he knew
it. It's one more thing they had in common.

She broke it off with that teacher. Later he became a
state assemblyman. Janet saw a campaign poster of him
stuck in someone's lawn. He looked good. Even more handsome; he wore a tie. She'd never thought to insist he wear
one; she had been so sure he looked best tieless. He posed
with a wife and two kids. She'd never heard him talk about
either a wife or kids. The wife looked long-suffering, not
fresh and new, and the kids were high-school-age, though
Janet had been the man's lover four years ago. Five, tops.
Oh, the havoc she could wreak with a simple phone call. But
it wasn't her style. And if anything, that he'd kept a secret
like that made him more interesting.

The spring storms were harsh that year. She watched Dave tame the weather and it thrilled her more now that she knew what he was like. When he told the region not to be afraid of this unusual weather, she felt like he was saying it just for her.

The mousy woman stopped leaving in the mornings; now she came and went all day, and her car occupied a guest parking slot, which, Janet noted, now had a number on it instead of *Guest*. As spring became summer and jackets were shed, Janet observed, happily, that the woman had gotten fat. Janet was certain Dave would dump her now, until she realized the woman wasn't fat, but pregnant.

o o o

On the last day of summer, Janet smelled smoke as she sunbathed in her backyard. She stood up, sniffed and stretched, and saw Dave pacing his yard, sucking frantically at a cigarette. She skipped over to her fence and tippy-toed on the wooden ledge that ran along the bottom so her chest was visible and she could rest her arms casually along the top.

"I didn't know you smoked," she called over. Dave jumped as if her words were a hot prod. He regarded her and then the cigarette with shame.

"I don't."

Janet tugged at the strings of her bikini top nonchalantly, jiggling her breasts. He wasn't looking. "What's with the cigarette then?"

"Janet," he said, as in *not now*.

But yes, now, she thought, and began to tingle. She waited a beat. "I'm not going anywhere."

He shook his head. "It's embarrassing."

She smiled. "I'm good with embarrassing."

He stared at her suspiciously, then shyly. He sighed. "My wife is so pregnant. We can't. You know."

Wife? When did that happen? Janet winced, but recovered quickly.

She snorted. "Oh, you're just not trying. Get creative."

"No," he said sharply, and then flatly, "I'm trying. I really am. It's just not happening."

Janet nodded. She could work with this. She pictured his wife, that small awkward woman, lying limp on a bed, her belly jutting up like a hill in a prairie. Janet's stomach turned. She wouldn't do that woman either. She imagined Dave in the corner, tugging furiously but still soft, regarding the mound with disgust. "Maybe I can help."

"Help?" he snapped, and then, as if a wind had pushed her scent to him, he all at once noticed her: her sunbathing bikini, her glistening skin, hair tied with studied messiness, the anonymity of her behind sunglasses. She could be anybody he wanted her to be. And she could be it now. He drifted over to his fence and stepped up onto the ledge so they were face to face. His eyes moistened. Janet cupped her breasts.

He said, "Oh."

o o o

Dave arrived a few minutes later, his summery baseball cap in front of his waist, sheepish, irresistibly everyman. Janet already lay across the bed, propped on her elbows, flipping through a magazine. The bedspread clung to her skin, which was moist with tanning oil. She waved her feet in the air, rolled onto her side, and hiked her hip dramatically.

"You don't mind?" he asked dumbly.

"Mind?"

She thought he'd never stop hovering in the doorway, watching her roll around on her bed. Boredom flashed through her veins. Stretching so her back arched and her breasts slid from their little bikini homes, she ordered, "Get over here."

In the middle of their first time he whimpered gratefully in a way that made her sick. Sick to have a man on top of her who was not hollering and talking dirty, and also sick to think there was something Dave Santana could do that would ruin him for her. He seemed lost. She hated lost.

"Say your name."

"Huh?" he grunted, slowing his pumping.

"Say your name."

He lifted slightly so he could look at her. "Dave?"

"Say your whole name," she cried, tugging on his hips to keep going.

"Dave Santana," he said haltingly.

"No, Dave. Say it all. Say 'I'm Meteorologist Dave Santana,' " she begged, sucking his lip.

In a confused daze, he said it quietly. Then he said it again. On the third time, his voice boomed, and he hoisted her hips up roughly and pumped deeper with each word he yelled. "I'm Meteorologist Dave Santana! I'm Meteorologist Dave Santana! I'm Meteorologist Dave Santana!" He came hard and tense, like a bus driver slamming the brakes. Janet seized with pleasure in the midst of all of the delicious commotion. In her head she repeated happily, *You're my match, you're my equal.*

After the sixth time Janet lay sore, wasted, and ecstatic. "Is it always like this?" she asked, reveling in so much shared wetness.

"Ha! No way. Never before," he said, still panting. "This guy must really like you." He wagged his exhausted penis with his thumb and middle finger.

Janet forced a giggle, even though she hated when men talked about their dicks like people.

"No, it's usually different," he continued, splayed on the bed and dreamy-voiced. "Because we're in love." He added quickly, "Me and the wife."

"Naturally." Janet felt uncharacteristically embarrassed. I know you don't mean me, she thought resentfully.

He clasped her hand like they were kids about to run across a field together, gave it a squeeze. "You're fun, Janet." He half smiled; it seemed flirtatious and challenging in a way that quickened her breath.

"Tell me something I don't know," she challenged back. She meant it. She wanted to hear a real thing, a thing only he could say. Even if it was lame, like how she tasted. Even if it was really about him, like how she felt to fuck.

His half smile faded, then became a frown, as he thought. She heard the muffled tick of Dave's watch from under the tangled sheets.

Finally, he coughed meekly. "I should go." Guilt tainted his voice. "Meredith will be home soon. Mommy class."

Her name is Meredith, Janet thought. She faked a yawn to protect the small wound she felt opening in her. "Come back anytime," she sang in a practiced tone, inviting, yet nonchalant.

"I think that should get me through. Like a dose of medicine, you know?"

"It was six doses," she teased, but felt hollow.

He chuckled gamely, then was silent as he finished dressing.

The low sun poured orange through the window. The whole room filled to spilling with it.

Dave came to the bed. "Thanks," he said, and extended a hand for her to shake. Janet eyed it until he withdrew the hand, wiped it on his pant leg.

"Janet." He sounded disappointed, as though he thought she was ruining this. He was now unsure how to leave.

She posed on the bed seductively out of habit, but she didn't know how to feel.

"Well, I'm always here," she said.

"I know. You're always here." He sighed. "You're hard to ignore."

She should like this comment, but coming from him it sounded like an accusation, as if displaying her dogged desire was somehow unfair. She *was* always there. She had guessed this kind of attention would be hard for Dave to ignore no matter who he belonged to. And she'd been right. It's not easy being pursued. That was the point. When all goes well, the wondering gives way to the wanting, then to the needing. These were the stages in the kind of seduction she was best at. He wasn't supposed to know why he came to her, to be able to parse the logic, to weigh his options, to have an opinion even. He was just supposed to come. But she could see him deciding a mistake had been made. He was feeling duped. She felt like a bad magician who had messed up. The audience had seen the con, the manipulation, and could never unsee it.

She rolled onto her back and began pushing her breasts toward the center of her chest, then letting them slip back down toward her armpits. It was the least sexy thing she'd ever done in front of a man. Dave Santana averted his eyes.

o o o

Since her brother Jon and his wife Gloria had their first kid, they'd insisted Janet have Sunday brunches with them once a month. "I want a normal family," Jon said. Janet had grown to dislike her brother. She found Gloria to be overly housewifely. Their union seemed like happenstance, as did the baby. Like they'd just floated out of state college and hooked fingers to keep floating together. How could they think that was worthwhile? Where was the passion, the anguish, the power play? Had Jon learned nothing from her?

"When are you going to find someone?" her brother asked, ten minutes into the visit. She always hated the question, and he always asked it.

"I don't know, Jon. When are *you* going to find someone?" she spat back, glaring at Gloria, who was pouring tea. Gloria looked confused for a moment, opened her mouth as if to explain, *He* did *find someone—me*, but then she understood it had been mean-spirited. Wide-eyed, she excused herself to the kitchen, calling Jon in to help. He jumped up and held the baby out to Janet. She made no move to uncross her arms.

"Come on. Don't tell me you don't want to hold him."

He slacked his arms and the baby seemed to free-fall, then abruptly stop to dangle at Jon's knees. Janet cringed, afraid he'd let baby head hit marble coffee table. "Why won't you settle down?" he asked, changing the subject but acting as if they were one and the same.

Janet said, "I *am* settled down."

"Oh?" Jon sat again. "You've been seeing someone?"

"Yes. The *meteorologist*."

"Janet." Jon rolled his eyes. "He probably just thinks you're a groupie."

"Thanks."

"You know how you get."

"For your information," Janet said, "we've been *seeing* each other quite a while." It wasn't exactly a lie. It *felt* that way to her, though three nights over a couple of years wouldn't seem like that to anyone else. Despite how their last encounter had ended, she missed him. She wanted him to knock on her door and was feeling depressed that he hadn't. She liked this game with her brother of pretending that he had.

Janet made up some details and dished them like gossip. The more she said, the more her brother believed. Dave took her to fancy restaurants; people asked for his autograph, and he obliged gracefully. He told her secrets through his weather reports, "Like when he says 'wind gusts,' he's telling me he loves me."

"Wow," Jon said, truly admiring.

She felt inspired. "He said I was the woman he'd been waiting for. And can you believe it—we were neighbors. He was right there the whole time. Just like that song."

Gloria kept calling Jon from the kitchen, but he was rapt. "I knew you could do it," he said, his eyes glistening. He touched Janet's arm.

She'd just been about to wonder, Why is he so happy for me? She was winning this fight, after all—she was saying whatever she could to prove him wrong about her life, her ability to find love. But something buckled in her at his touch, a transference of emotion or of belief. And she began to believe it herself. Believe in the possibility. Maybe it *could* work. Maybe she *could* do it.

Finally Gloria came out, hands on her hips, and barked, "Are you fucking deaf? Get the fuck in here." Jon bolted up and dropped the baby into Janet's lap. And Janet, too stunned by Gloria's outburst, a kind she'd never thought Gloria capable of, automatically wrapped her arms around the warm squirming mass, as if it were second nature. His head smelled like old furniture no one wanted. "What is the point of you?" she asked, looking him squarely in the eyes. He rolled his head back and forth, like someone in ecstasy.

o o o

The mulch around the front windows of Dave's town house was oversprinklered. Fall decay clung to her slippers. She still hadn't seen Dave, even though she'd been looking for him. If she wanted to get under his skin, she'd need to be more proactive. She'd thought up a line: "You said I didn't need to be scared of weather. Then why is everything *dying*?" She'd also brought a measuring cup with her, in case his wife was there. Neighbors still did that, right? Not that she cared, but she had grown so tired of people regarding her with suspicion. She'd won another award at school, and the other teachers complained she was rigging it. Please, she thought. She had better things to do than tamper with school elections. I wished I'd gotten the memo ordering us to stop making a difference, she'd said to her girls in Sex Ed. They applauded, and when she asked that they not vote for her next year, they refused. She admired their conviction.

A ficus showered Janet as she brushed past to spy into the window. The blinds were drawn, and she could not see inside. Maybe his wife was still pregnant. How long had it been? It seemed like just last week. She could still taste his sea-saltiness. Maybe, she daydreamed, his wife would even approve—would motion for Janet to follow her into the house, saying, "Please take him. He makes me so sick," then opening the bathroom door to reveal him wet and grunt-ing, beating off over the toilet. He'd see Janet and exclaim, "Thank God you're here!" Janet could take him back to her place, and he would explode inside her, and then afterward maybe they would talk. He'd see she was the better woman because she always knew how to fix his problems. Maybe he would never leave. Maybe he'd visit his baby from her town house. Actually, she couldn't think of a more convenient situation, it being just next door.

She knocked, measuring cup ready, and waited. She knocked again. It wasn't that late. Were they out? His car was gone. Was hers? She tried the door, and it opened.

The living room was empty except for a rotary phone, lonely in the middle of the awful mauve carpet; its cord slithered to the wall. Each door she opened led to a room empty of every remnant of him. The smell of food, sweat, his cologne, clung to the surfaces. The breeze through the door churned it all up for her.

On the kitchen counter she found the sales binder, though it was already clear Dave had moved. Moved *secretly*, Janet marveled, feeling both angry and intrigued. So she wouldn't know. Because he couldn't face her? Because he was ashamed? Because he didn't want to hurt her? Because he *did* want to hurt her? All of these possibilities excited her.

At the association office, the clerk eyed her soggy slippers when she inquired.

"They moved a couple weeks ago. Weren't you at the party?" he answered innocently. She could tell this guy, name-tagged Jeremy, disliked her.

"What party?"

"Their going-away party. Maybe two weeks ago? In their yard."

She'd probably been at her brother's. "That bastard," she muttered about both men and tore a card for an association-approved landscaper into ragged pieces.

Jeremy's eyes slit. "You live here?" he asked, as though there was no way she could have not known about the party, let alone not attend, if she did.

"Yes, I live here," she snapped. "I've lived here since the beginning. Since before you."

He flipped casually through a binder. "Well, their little girl is cute. Had an adorable golden curl on her forehead. Perfection. Like a picture of a baby. But a real baby."

She slammed her keys onto the counter. "I'm also putting my house on the market," she said, trying to sound nonchalant and failing.

"Oh?" He brightened as if glad.

"You know, I've come in here before."

"Yes," he nodded, smiling. "I remember." His smile was flat, a stain. "Then you know that you can go through the association's agent or find your own." He pushed some pamphlets at her. "Buyers have to come here first. No signs in the window or on the lawn. It's tacky. There's a fine." So Dave hadn't been stealthy, he'd just been following rules. He hadn't run from her; he'd simply moved to a new home, started a new life, and hadn't thought to tell her. On a corkboard over Jeremy's head hung four flyers picturing four almost identical town houses. She recognized Dave's because of the weather vane he'd installed. She'd found it so charming; now it seemed stupid. She thought of that empty mauve carpeting.

"I tore up all my carpet and put in real wood floors, so I imagine mine will sell pretty quickly. A lot quicker than these pieces of shit," she said, gesturing at the board.

"I imagine so," Jeremy agreed, his gaze calm but alert, as if he'd encountered a strange dog in the forest. "Wood flooring is very timeless right now."

"We used to sleep together." She dropped it like an oily chicken.

"I'm sorry?"

"Dave and I. Before he was married. After he was married. While she was pregnant." She smiled. "We were lovers. Multiple times. Multiple orgasms, I mean." She paused. What *did* she mean exactly? "I mean, I *know* him. *I* know him."

She stopped. She didn't need to plead her case to *Jeremy*.

"I'm sure you do." He sighed. "Please let someone in the office know what you decide." He turned his back to her. "And you should have shoes on," he added, disappearing behind a curtain. "It's almost winter."

o o o

Another family moved into Dave's place. Janet saw ribbons of old carpet in the Dumpster and figured they had installed hardwood floors. She decided Dave had bad taste and added that to her growing list of his failings. She watched the husband over the fence as he staked the yard according to some spring planting map. She thought about seducing him, but he was doughy, and worse, clearly under the wife's thumb. Janet pictured him barely erect and simpering at her bedside.

She did not try to sell.

But she continued to watch Dave's weather reports, the friendly hum of the vibrator mingling with his expert's voice. He'd developed something of a giggle that confused her at first, until she realized that it came with something of a smile, genuine, not slight, and ever-present. This was Dave happy. She hated seeing it; it made her want to cry. She masturbated angrily.

Then one day in early spring, with the ground still frozen and the night still arriving by five, the weather was reported by a blonde in a tight pencil skirt and bursting cleavage. Janet was eating cookies from a box in her bra and sweat pants, vibrator tucked under the elastic band, ready.

The broadcast confused Janet. The blonde hadn't said, "Filling in for Meteorologist Dave Santana." She'd called herself the weather girl. Janet tried, but she couldn't get off to that high voice, to an imagined smell rather than a known one.

In the morning, the paper announced a station shakeup. The only people who watched the weather were fishermen, and they wanted a weather girl.

And like that, Meteorologist Dave Santana was gone.

o o o

That year, Janet entertained no remarkable men. Those who woke next to her were proud to confess some shortcoming, as though vulnerability was a new trend. She hated the fears most of all; "I fear I'll never find someone who will love me for me," said a landscaper, who played guitar in a local 1970s cover band. You probably won't, Janet would think as he clung to her. But admittedly she had softened, and mostly she kept her mouth shut, or if she ventured to respond, pointedly sighed. She sighed a lot post-Dave.

Worse, she thought she saw Meredith Santana everywhere. At the gas station pumping gas, with a baby in a car seat. Or at the supermarket, a baby strapped to her back. At the bar where Janet picked up game men, bouncing a baby on her knee and flirting in a frayed booth. Squinting out from the background of the adult movies Janet watched. The woman was a specter toting a specter child. Janet wasn't sure she even remembered what Meredith looked like. She only recalled pregnant Meredith, and so couldn't even remember, or had never known, if she was as naturally thin as Janet.

So when Meredith Santana walked into the teachers'

lounge, there to cover the school nurse's maternity leave, Janet barely had any surprise left in her.

Meredith was nothing like Janet remembered. She was lovely. She wore her shining brown hair in a stylish blunt cut; she was athletic and obviously naturally thin. Her appeal wasn't fleeting; she would always turn heads. Janet couldn't believe it was the same woman she'd seen slinking off mornings a few years ago. Maybe she had been transformed by the power of Dave's love for her. When Meredith shook her hand, Janet held it uncomfortably long, then reached out to pinch Meredith's arm, to test that her flesh was real. Meredith jerked her hand away, eyed Janet, but then laughed. An easygoing girl, the kind who fits herself in anywhere and easily belongs.

Janet avoided speaking to Meredith after that. But when they were both in the lounge, Janet couldn't help but register the fact. She listened for Meredith's voice over all others, or for the mention of her name in gossip. She found herself skulking outside the nurse's office. She parked two spaces beyond Meredith's car so she would need to walk by it twice a day. She chose the pasta because Meredith chose the pasta; likewise, the meatloaf, the pizza, the wet ham for her salad. In the small, sallow fitness room at school, Janet watched Meredith StairMaster, mesmerized by the shifting apples of her ass, Janet's mouth shamefully agape.

One day Meredith walked into Janet's room during a prep period and slid into a front-row desk usually occupied by her worst student, the quiet flutist.

"It seems like you've been following me," Meredith said, serene as a cat.

What balls, Janet thought. She found it difficult to speak. She could only open and close her mouth silently. "I'm not," she finally croaked.

"Look," Meredith continued kindly but firmly, "I've only heard things, so forgive me if I'm out of line. But I'm married." She added, "To a man."

Janet would have laughed had she not almost sobbed. She couldn't explain that her obsession with Meredith stemmed from the need to know what Dave truly desired, or why it wasn't her. There had to be a clue.

Janet recovered slightly. "I know you're married. I *know* him."

"Oh?" Meredith said brightly, sitting up in her chair. "How do you know Dave?"

Janet prepared herself for the mayhem, but Meredith's inviting smile stalled her. *She should be suspicious. I should be a threat.* Janet felt powerless. She gasped slightly. She couldn't do it. And she couldn't believe she couldn't do it.

Meredith covered for her. "He was the weatherman—that's how."

"You mean meteorologist," Janet said, trying to reprimand her. Janet would never make that mistake.

"Oh, shame on me. He was the *meteorologist.*" She laughed it off easily. "Now he gives motivational speeches." She beamed, as though unaware that the teachers talked endlessly about her locally famous husband. She probably was unaware. She was the kind of blessed person to whom love, happiness, family, security, confidence, beauty, were just what came with normal old life. She'd probably been told to expect it all.

"I saw him motivate once," Janet riddled quietly to herself. It was all she could muster. She wanted to curl up under her desk.

Then Meredith leaned in conspiratorially, said, "I know he's no movie star, but he had fans. Women writing letters. Waiting outside the station. He had this neighbor once. He said—oh, I can't," she said, dissolving into giggles.

He had told Meredith about her. But how much? Not everything, since they were still together. Right? Couldn't be everything, because she was laughing. Right? How much did married people talk about?

Meredith waved her hand. "But I *get* it. I stalked him too!" She nodded vehemently, her eyes wide and girl-talky. "I did!" she squealed. "I finagled an invite to a party he was at. I wouldn't let him talk to any other women. Oh, did I flirt! I was *shameless*," she insisted. "*Those eyes*." Now they were married, and had a beautiful daughter. "And," she said, patting her flat belly, "another on the way." She put her finger to her lips. "Shh. Secret."

Janet was flustered. Obsession did pay off. Just not for her. Meredith was the magician. She slumped. "I wasn't following you," she lied morosely.

Meredith waved her hand. "Oh, pooh, I don't know why I thought that. I let silly lounge gossip get the better of me."

What had she heard? Could be any number of things. Janet winced. Since when did she care?

"You know," Meredith said, "the teachers here, they're so prim. I couldn't tell them that story. But I think we're probably similar." She was smiling at Janet in such a genuine way, with the openness, the small-scale arousal that comes from meeting someone just like you. "We should hang out."

Janet stood and moved things around on her desk, cycloning them into a shape. She should go home with Meredith Santana, cozy herself into the couch with wine, laugh like best girlfriends, and be there when Dave walked in. She should cross the room to him, squeeze his surprised hand, and say, "I loved your work," or "I still need my meteorologist," and play it off like it's what any cheeky at-home watcher would say, wink at Meredith, make her laugh, get her on her side. She could make Meredith love her so that Dave cracked. She knew she could. Her mind screamed, Do it! Wreck it! Ruin it all! She tasted bile. "I'm late," she sputtered and threw a stapler into her bag.

Meredith glanced at the school clock. It was still thirty minutes before the next period. "For what?"

Janet shook her head. "I'm just too late." She left.

Sitting in the car in front of her town house, Janet scolded herself. She'd let a moment pass. Since when was what she wanted not part of the plan? She let the tears come. She'd succumbed to this new era of sentimentality and weakness, in which possibility was dead and buried and there were actually some things *you just don't do*.

o o o

Though she knew Meredith was a temporary fill-in who, most likely, would not return after summer, Janet arranged a transfer to the high school in the next town over. With her awards she easily convinced them to make room for her on the faculty. Her female students wept. Some promised to transfer. But she said, "Stay put, do well, don't get pregnant. For me." The teachers in the lounge peppered her with questions that feigned concern. Is everything all right? Family emergency? Hidden secret? As a last gasp at insult, she just smiled and said she wanted something better for herself. Still, they offered her cookies more readily than they ever had before. Meredith, oblivious, genuinely wished her luck, her hand absentmindedly protecting the growing Santana in her belly.

In her new school, Janet ran through the single men, and some of the married ones, finally settling on a well-built phys ed teacher who had no idea that he should have striven for more. He didn't mind her gray hairs that popped up here, there. Her older breasts weren't as pert, but he still thought she was sexy when she bounced astride him, and this had an effect on her; it filled her with a terrible feeling of gratitude. The phys ed teacher was a solid lover, and she inched down closer to his level. The sex ranged from fine to good, more tender than wild or frightening. It was nothing like with Dave Santana, but she'd known, during those too-brief encounters, that would likely be the case. She was at her best with electrifying men.

She and the phys ed teacher settled into something surprisingly monogamous, though they remained unmarried. Eventually they forgot why they'd wanted to hide their relationship at school and began timing their lunch break to sit at the same table. They spent nights at each other's house, each stashing their belongings in an emptied drawer of the other's dresser. She met his aunt. She'd never met a lover's aunt before. Occasionally they drove to school together. But neither mentioned wanting more. Janet dreaded that conversation, but also couldn't help wondering why it never came.

o o o

A little girl shrieked at a man in the diner, horrified in the way children often are; big tears for small problems. Janet cupped her ears dramatically, scowled in their direction. But then, the slump of the man's shoulders, the squatness of his neck, the beige; she knew it was Dave without even seeing his face. And if there were any doubt, his likeness marred the towheaded little girl with long curling pigtails; beyond the raging tantrum lay that same blankness. Janet's stomach flipped.

She slid out of her booth and sidled up to him and his daughter.

The girl regarded her warily when Janet drew a line down Dave's back with her finger, playfully accusing, "I *know* you."

Dave's back arched away from her finger instinctively. He turned and for a second—she saw it in his eyes—wondered who she was.

"It's the hair," she said, fluffing the ends of her now shorter bob, mildly flustered. The girl's big eyes darted from Janet to Dave and back, narrowing into slits. Dave's own eyes narrowed, remembering.

"Janet." He adjusted his windbreaker. "Well," he said curtly.

"I miss you on TV, Dave," she growled. His mildness made her feel predatory. She wanted to drop to her knees, suck him in front of the entire dinner crowd.

"Well, you know I haven't been on television for some time, Janet." Being with the phys ed teacher, she'd gotten used to a certain standard of the male form that Dave had never possessed. But he was trimmer than the last time she'd seen him, looked a little more rugged—was that a tan?—a little more ready for anything.

"You look good, Dave," she flirted, and waited for him to respond in kind. He did not.

"You know, Dave, I miss you other places too."

He bent down and fidgeted with his daughter's back-pack. The girl wiggled away from him.

Janet tried a new tactic. "You know, Dave, I met your wife a couple years ago."

"No, you didn't," he said, flashing anger, certain he had kept his worlds apart.

She had always liked being someone's secret, but it was clear being known held more power. "Yes. I did. She was a nurse in my school."

His face tightened with ugly anxiety. A face, she realized, he'd made often, when reporting on the nicest, balmiest weather or all those nor'easters, while being seduced, when he came. She pictured the face in some confessional moment with his wife. But no. He would never. Would he?

"Don't worry," she said, disgusting herself by backing down.

The cashier called his name. "Stay there, Hannah," he barked.

"Hannah," Janet cooed. "That's a good girl's name. Are you a good girl?"

Hannah shook her head and pouted.

"You know, Hannah, the last time I saw you, you were in your mommy's belly. And how old are you now?"

"Five," the girl said, her eyes big and wet.

Janet nodded, bored by the information, and smoothed her own hair, let her hand trail down her body to rest on her hip, hoping Dave would notice. But it was the girl who watched. She mimicked the move.

How adorable, Janet thought. She reached out and fondled one of the girl's pigtails, silky like a dog's ear. She coiled it around her finger and gave it a sharp tug. The girl winced and then stared at her with a mysterious smile. If I were a man, Janet mused, I'd insist on a paternity test.

"You remind me of me," she whispered to the girl.

Hannah curtsied, then said, "You're ugly."

Janet clapped, delighted. She tugged both pigtails, and the girl succumbed to the move, the tension on her scalp pleasurable. It took Janet's breath away.

Dave returned, swatted at Janet's hand. "Please stop touching my daughter's hair."

"If you insist," she said, and reached for his hair instead.

"Janet. Please." He ducked her. "It's not a good time," he muttered, ushering the girl to the door.

What could that mean? She felt giddy. Dave's got a problem? "I'll always be there for you. And I know you know where to find me," she called, and he paused, just briefly. She could see a tension—the good kind, she thought—pulse down his back. From his stuttered step, Janet thrillingly anticipated the ruin of everything. She wanted him to scold her again. Then half smile in the way she liked. She would know that he couldn't forget, was haunted by her in the same way she was by him. Maybe he'd ended up with what he *really* wanted, but there had been moments when Janet had clouded the picture. And she could do it again. She'd just done it. He would think of her tonight. She knew it. Then strangely, shamefully, she wanted to take it back. Her offer felt false, and yet she'd said it. Was that what she *really* wanted? More of that? Or did she want something new? She hated all this dry thinking. In a daze, Janet shuffled over to the window.

Dave unlocked his car, and his little girl lifted the back door handle, needing all her strength to pull it open. The girl climbed into the car seat, and Dave buckled her in, tenderly now that they were alone.

Maybe it wouldn't be so bad to have a child who was just like her. It would be a place to put what Janet knew. All of it. And children bring other, unexpected things. Certain perks. Maybe Meredith and Dave hadn't fallen quickly in love, as much as their lust begat a baby that began their family. Janet hadn't considered lapsing on birth control to get Dave's attention. She'd assumed what life had to offer wouldn't require compromises. And a child had always felt like the biggest compromise. But the strings attached didn't have to be bad strings, did they? Strings might have secured a good life. Strings might have tied her to Dave. If she'd played this wrong, she could make up for it easily enough, couldn't she? Whenever Dave showed up at her door, hat in hand. If he showed.

Or.

Maybe she could secure that life tonight, when her phys ed teacher arrived with wine and a roast chicken from the supermarket.

Or maybe they could just talk about it.

You can always change your mind, Janet thought with an ache as she watched that little Santana girl turn toward her. Behind the car window, she made what looked like a kissing face and wiggled it all around. Janet blushed and blew a childish kiss back. But then the girl pinched her nose, and Janet could see that in reality there had been no affection; the girl had been making a scrunched, sour, taunting face all along. *You stink*, was what she meant.

FLOTSAM

"Linda means 'beautiful' in Spanish," the man in her bed whispers.

"My name is Lydia," she whispers back.

○ ○ ○

In the morning he is sitting on her kitchen counter drinking a beer, his ankle crossed over his knee, his belt buckle still dangling, his mustache glistening from some unknown wetness.

"I thought you'd be gone," says Lydia.

"I mean to be." He gulps the last of the beer and walks past her, pinching her ass on the way out.

While folding laundry, she finds a tiny blue sock that isn't hers and wonders if the man left it accidentally and it shrank in the wash, or if he left it and his feet (or at least one of them) are amazingly petite. She can't remember his feet. His name might have been Raul.

The next week, she finds a small red mitten in with her whites, the wool felted from the hot water wash. It could have shrunk, she thinks, remembering the particular style of

Doug, with his crisped shiny hair, his colorful thigh tattoo. It could be a fashion statement. But it is late May; the time for wool mittens is over.

Next, a small pumpkin-colored T-shirt appears in the dryer, *Billy* stitched in blue thread across the tiny chest. The neck is so small she cannot get her head through. Could it have shrunk too?

"Is this yours?" She holds it up for the man eating a Pop-Tart at her table, who studies the shirt from his chair.

"No," he says finally. "My name is John."

○ ○ ○

On her bed, she lays out a small empty child with the clothes from weeks of laundry. Little Billy's orange T-shirt, the blue sock and the mitten on the right, a pink ruffled girl's sock for the left foot. A pair of blue jean overalls, from Sears, size L, 3 to 5 years. A corduroy jacket—the most recent find— with patches from Disney World and Lionel Trains sewn on with mismatched thread.

The variations in size give the empty child a disfigured look.

She fingers the T-shirt material, and it is too soft. The lack of friction irritates her, like rubbing two chalk-covered fingers together. She picks up the jacket. Who sews patches onto clothing anymore? Who plays with trains? She picks at the thread and the patch loosens from the fabric. The exposed corduroy looks brand new and is soft like velvet.

She's hoping Frank will stay the night, but it would be bad for him to see this.

She gathers the clothes into a black plastic bag, intending

to throw it away, but instead places it in the corner of the kitchen nearest to the laundry room. That night, she hustles Frank straight to her bedroom. "You sure know what you want," he says as she's flipping open his belt.

o o o

She sorts a frilly robin's-egg-blue girl's dress from a load of towels and storms into the kitchen, where Cal is standing in front of the open refrigerator.

"Don't you have anything stronger than milk?" he asks.

She throws the dress at him, and it lands quietly at his feet. "You planted this in my dryer."

He picks up the dress. "No, hon, it's not my size." He smirks, holding the dress against his bare chest. He begins to waltz with it. "La da dee," he hums. The hem caresses his navel, and the top just covers his left pec.

"This isn't a game," she says, folding her arms and gazing out the window sternly like she's seen in movies when women put their foot down about something. "Get out."

She waits until his car revs down the street before sitting down to eat the toast points she carefully cut the way he likes, dipping them in jam and chewing them with disgust. She doubts Cal will be back. She's only known him for a few weeks, but she will miss him. She spits a chewed toast point onto the plate.

o o o

For a while she keeps her laundry to a minimum, wearing the same underwear for days to avoid finding some unwanted article of clothing in with her delicates. But now she is washing every towel she uses, every bra and pair of socks and jeans, every blouse she wears each day. Just to see. And each day some tiny article of clothing emerges with her clean clothes. The pale blue turtleneck with a sleepy turtle stitched on the front. The little T-shirt with the grass stain on the sleeve. The sweater emblazoned with a rainbow. Striped athletic socks. Superhero underwear. Clothes belonging to children named Patrick, Anna, Ned, Stacy, Jack, Heather.

o o o

The bag is stretched to the point of bursting, and she can't keep her eyes off it.

Her dad pours her another glass of wine and then wiggles the bottle in front of her face. He likes to bring nice wine when he comes for dinner.

She licks the corner of her napkin, absently reaches up to wipe away the wine he dribbled down his chin.

"Want me to take the garbage out?" he asks, following her gaze to the trash bag in the corner.

She shakes her head. "No," she says. "I'll do it." She picks up the bag and drags it upstairs, nestling it into the corner of her room where the dog bed used to sit, cozy between two curtained windows.

He's reaching across the table, cutting her steak, when she returns. She pushes the plate closer to him, and he helps himself.

"I'm thinking of getting an alarm system," she announces, though she hasn't been.

"Why?"

"The neighborhood is going down the toilet."

He looks out the window, expecting to see some crime in progress. Across the street, the neighbors still have Christmas lights in their evergreen shrubs, though it is summer. He takes this as a sign and nods in agreement.

That night she watches the bag in the corner. When car headlights sweep across it, and the neighbor's Christmas lights blink on the shiny black plastic, the bag looks as if it's squirming.

o o o

Cal is back to test the waters. Afterward he palms the sweat from his hairless chest, wipes it on the sheet beneath them, and points to the bag.

"What's in that?"

"Children's clothing."

"Lydia," he groans, "I thought we were on the same page."

"We are."

"So you're just collecting kids' clothes for fun?"

"No."

"Are you opening a store?"

"I'm not."

"So it's junk?"

"I guess so."

"Then get rid of it."

She nestles into him for warmth. It's good he's here.

"I will."

o o o

Early in the morning, when it is still dark and Cal is gently whimpering beneath a dream, she wrestles the bag down the stairs, then into the backseat of her car. It is surprisingly heavy and unwieldy, and her muscles shake under the strain.

In the rearview mirror she watches the bag. It sits tall and blank against the tan upholstery. She almost hits an old lady crossing the road. When she slams the brakes, the bag thumps against the back of her seat.

At the bridge over the big rushing river, she again wrestles the bag. She rests it on the cold metal railing, and it balances there, the wind seeming to hold it up from all sides. Then she barely touches the bag and it goes over the rail.

When the bag lands, the water closes in, submerging it. Then it bursts through the surface again like it's gasping for air. The light twinkles all over it, and she's surprised by how pretty it looks, like something special being showcased in a store window. She wonders if she should have kept it.

The bag floats away, and a few birds give chase. Their dawn shadows weave playfully as they swoop at the bag, and Lydia is glad they have found it. They'll know what to do. They're following some instinct that has to do with morning.

A WANTED MAN

There once was a man, a well-known man, we'll call him "our man," who could impregnate fifty women in one day.

He could bend a high-heeled dancer over a Dumpster; a waitress across the order counter; a teacher over the hood of her car in the teachers' lot. You get the picture. He could have any woman he wanted, anywhere he wanted. He could take one and turn, find another waiting, and take her too. We've all heard the stories. Remember how he did a row of bank tellers, one after the other? How they begged and huffed and grunted, their faces pressed against their teller windows where they'd stuck a Closed sign when it was their turn? "We're so lucky!" they squealed. Remember how they all took maternity leave at the same time? Remember the elevator story? That Little League game? Independence Day?

Our man was in his prime, his status secure. His off-spring were the most coveted, the most successful, he was a sure thing—he never missed, and he was always ready (which can't be said of lesser men). Women dreamed of having his babies. Young boys dreamed of being him. Other men knew to keep their distance and their eyes down.

But our man believed all of that was changing.

Impossible, you say? As proof, take that waitress story: When he'd bent her over the counter, the cooks had tried to ambush him. The waitress held them off with a kitchen knife, and they'd had to finish over the prep table, with her holding the knife out, jabbing it at the cooks with each thrust our man gave her.

Our man recognized the look in the cooks' eyes. They were thinking, That should be me. He knew the feeling. For some young men it was a long-held life goal, and for others it came out of nowhere like a punch. They wanted what he had, and so deeply that they believed they could get it, should get it. They deserved it.

Lately young men had been ambushing our man from dark alleys, following him home, breaking into his apartment and setting traps. He'd had to move. Before, he would have walked unguarded and proud. Now he skulked and wore disguises. He saw the Wanted signs with his picture affixed.

But of all the changes, he was most bewildered by how much he wanted to see the waitress again.

Once they'd finished, he'd asked if she would like to sit with him, have a coffee, talk. He felt a heaviness in his stomach, a need to spend time with her. It was the strangest feeling—he'd never desired a woman twice. But she already had her order pad and pencil cocked and ready. "I work here," she'd said briskly, and returned to her tables. He'd blushed and felt ashamed. When was the last time he'd felt that?

Now he thought of the knife, of the way she'd jabbed. She hadn't been protecting him so much as her offspring. But still, the gesture touched him. He felt cared for. He hadn't felt that since he was a much younger man, but he wanted to feel it again.

o o o

Our man returned to the diner, anxious and prepared to ask the waitress to meet him after her shift. He would offer to buy her a sandwich or a soup at a different diner where she could relax. That was better than coffee, right?

But the waitress wasn't there. The cooks were, however, and they chased our man onto a dim side street, where he was able to lose them. He panted in a Dumpster until it was safe to emerge.

Our man knew of a cave in the big park near the diner. He could wait out the night and go back tomorrow, see if the waitress was working. Tell her he couldn't stop thinking about her. They could marvel at how weird that was. He had a feeling she would totally get it, and get him.

The sun was bright, and the grass smelled extra grassy because of it. Park animals scampered. Our man kept his head down, slipped behind trees and into bushes when threatening types strode by. He stepped over two different ankle traps he assumed were set for him.

He entered a wide-open space with few hiding spots. A crowd of boys on bikes noticed him. "Hey," they yelled. They lobbed stones at his head. Our man ran, and the boys chased on their bikes through the gravel paths. Of course it could only be a game for them—they were boys—but the commotion alerted others. An arrow was launched from somewhere in the trees, and it whizzed by our man's head. A large group of healthy young men began tracking him. But our man is faster than most.

He gained ground by sprinting over a steep hill, and then he heard a sweet voice say, "Pssst."

A woman in a yellow dress sat on a large blanket in the middle of the great lawn. She scooched over and lifted a corner. Our man dove under, and she laid it back down. She reclined so as to hide his bulk, then resumed reading her book with great languorousness.

Those pursuing our man crested the hill, breathless, and scanned the lawn for some movement. The woman yawned for effect. They ran on, fought with each other for the lead; the young boys were jostled off their bikes and limped away, crying bitterly, pining for the day they would feel like men.

When they were all out of sight, the woman tickled our man through the blanket, and he laughed.

"Shh, they're very close," she lied. She rubbed him until his breath quickened. "I'm taking you home with me. It's safe there."

Our man was happy to hear that. No one had ever offered him a home. He would stay with her, be cared for, and never have to run again.

She leaned and peeked under the blanket: her eyes shone like stained glass; her brown hair piled in the grass like curled dead leaves. His waitress was forgotten.

o o o

Our man woke to the woman snapping pictures of him; she'd tucked a flower behind his ear and was pretending to feed him grapes.

"My girlfriends are going to freak out." She giggled. "Can I invite them over?"

"I only want you." He grabbed her and tenderly kissed her cheeks, then her forehead, her eyes. "Let's get married," he said. He couldn't remember the last time he felt so safe.

"Oh, I can't." She fake pouted. "I'm already married."

"You are?"

She pulled away and snapped another picture.

"Run away with me then," he said. "We could find a new home together, somewhere no one knows me."

"Oh no, I couldn't."

It felt as if a chunk of ice was going down his throat. "Don't you love me?"

She laughed. "You funny man," she said, and tried to push his face between her legs.

The icy lump reached his heart, and then his stomach. It was a new sensation. He said, "But you want kids with me."

"I want your kid, not, 'I want to have kids with you.' It's different." She shrugged. "The kids my husband gave me stink. They're weak and they get terrible grades."

"You have kids?" He had no idea. "Where are they?"

"At my mom's." She sighed. "I don't know how much longer I get you for, and I don't want to waste it. Now, come on." She wiggled in his lap until he was ready.

o o o

Just as they finished, they heard the front door creak open, the sounds of a bag being tossed onto a table, papers in folders slapping down, and the tired sigh of someone who had no one to greet him.

"Hello? Anyone home?" a man called out.

"My husband's home." She groaned. "I was hoping for another go. It's so fun with you."

"Come with me then," he said as he threw clothes on.

She sulked. "No, that would probably ruin it."

They heard the husband pad around the apartment, into one room and then another, take something from the fridge, clink some glasses.

"Hello?" he called out again.

She jumped up to lock the bedroom door and barred it with her body. "I do love him," she said, but she looked at our man like she was eating something delicious. "It's complicated. Just be quiet for a minute. Maybe he'll go away."

The footsteps got closer. "Ellen?" the husband called out. "Are you in there?" The knob jiggled.

Our man began to tremble. "Let me out," he hissed. He didn't like being this close to a husband.

"Hey," the husband yelled. "Who's in there?"

Our man tossed Ellen aside and threw open the door.

He could tell the husband used to be handsome, but now he was older. His clothes were drab and hung on him poorly, his skin too; his hair was dyed shoe polish black to hide the gray.

The husband gasped, and our man recognized his look: as if a long-forgotten dream was resurfacing and giving him the wild idea to battle our man. It was folly. He was too old. But nostalgia and regret are powerful. He reached out.

Our man bolted past.

"Wait," the husband cried, lumbering after him. "Come back. Let's make a deal." But our man could hear him rummaging for weapons even as he tried to sound friendly.

Our man bounded from the apartment and took the stairs half a floor at a time.

"Dammit," the husband cried, and stomped his feet. He whined, "Ellen," and our man heard her respond, "It didn't mean anything." He felt that icy lump again.

○ ○ ○

Our man rushed through the streets, his head down, but still he felt like everyone was about to pounce. He ducked into a parking lot, squatted between two cars, and cried. The sky threatened rain. The buildings squatted sullenly. The lights in windows were green and harsh. The expressions on passersby were angry. They all seemed to be searching for something. Probably him.

"Um, hi?" said a shy voice.

Our man shrank against a car, frightened. How careless. He hadn't heard anyone approach; he could be facing his death right now.

A woman reached for him. "Don't be scared."

"What do you want?" he hissed, and blushed at how unkind it sounded. Where were his manners? She looked nice.

"This is my car," she said.

He laughed with some relief. "I'm sorry." He rose, though he remained hunched and averted from the crowded sidewalk.

"Are you okay?"

"I'm fine." He wiped his eyes. "Hard day."

"Don't I know it." She leaned where he had been leaning, and pulled a cigarette from her purse. She thoughtfully
exhaled, and our man felt hidden in her fog.

"Thank you," he said, relaxing a bit in her company.

"For what?"

"For just standing here with me."

She smiled. "I'm happy to. You look like you could use
a friend. I'm Jill." She extended her hand. "And you are?"

His breath halted, his tongue swelled: she didn't know
him.

She was plain looking, with straightened black hair,
small eyes, thin lips, but big rosy cheeks that made her
whole self inviting. She was the kind of woman he might
overlook. She seemed like a person who didn't want to be
seen. He wanted to be around someone like that forever.
Maybe he would grow plain then. Blend in. He'd like that.
He took her hand.

"Do you want to go somewhere?" He imagined her too
insecure and unassuming to ask herself.

She blushed, elated. "Sure?" She ducked her head in dis-
belief and gleeful shame. "I can't believe I'm doing this."
She hooked onto his arm and began to walk.

"Won't we take your car?" he asked, his hand on the
door.

"No, my place is just around the corner."

He concentrated on watching her so he wouldn't panic
on the sidewalk. He felt ordinary with this woman on his
arm, like he could look people in the eye. But he didn't dare.

o o o

Her apartment was bare, but still she searched awhile for mugs.

"Did you just move in?"

"Oh yeah," she said, now looking through drawers for tea.

"Where did you move from?" Our man sat on a spare wooden chair at an empty table.

"Uh, the Midwest?" she said scrunching her face at him as if she couldn't believe it herself. "I'd like to forget about that, honestly." Her voice swelled with emotion. He became aroused by her vulnerability.

"Well." He walked to her and gripped her hips. "You'll like it here."

She let him touch her, then demurred, put her mug between them. "Stop."

He raised his hands, surrendering. "I'm sorry." When was the last time he'd needed to say that?

"No—" She laughed, though with some sadness. She pushed his arms down to his sides. "It's just that I don't know anything about you."

He was flattered and thrilled. "What do you want to know?"

She opened her mouth like she would speak but didn't. He badly wanted to slip his thumb between those lips, have her gently tongue it. The silence between them rushed into his ears. He was scared to fill it. He felt dumb in her presence. But he wanted her to know him. "I'm lonely," he said.

She bowed her head, kissed his knuckles.

The tension in his shoulders released. He didn't know

when he'd felt such tenderness. Then he laughed, overjoyed. She laughed. They clasped hands and laughed together.

"I've always wanted a family," he said.

"Me too," she cooed.

"A real one, though. One I can watch grow." He skimmed his finger above her waistband, under her shirt. "I've never told anyone that."

She shivered and licked her lips. He thought, Here's the future, so why wait?

He got down on a knee and tied the string from his tea bag around her finger.

"Will you marry me?" He couldn't believe he had said it. He imagined waking on a sun-dazzled morning with her.

She jogged in place and screamed, "Yes!"

He scooped her into his arms as if she were a long, light pillow. "You'll have to return to the Midwest," he said, and when she looked confused, he explained, "It's not safe for me here."

She cupped his face. "You're safe with me anywhere." Her eyes were wet and searching. "Do you feel safe?"

"I do feel safe! I felt safe the very first minute," he said, forgetting that in fact, he had felt in danger when he'd first encountered her.

He spun her in a circle. "I've got you and I won't ever let go," he cried, and she tossed her head and fluttered her legs like she was a captive in a monster movie. This time he wouldn't have to run.

The bedroom was also bare, a mattress on the floor with a single sheet balled at the foot. The windows were shrouded in brown cloth, but a chair had been placed where someone could sit and look out a crack between the fabric panels. There was a shabby painted dresser. Our man swiped what little was on it to the floor.

He pulled her shirt over her head; her breasts, oblong and heavy, spilled from her bra with just a flick of the straps. She was plump. Her belly looked strangely swollen. All evidence to the contrary, he might have guessed she was already pregnant. But no, she had the hunger of an empty woman.

She moaned she was ready, and she was. He was about to bend her over that dresser when she said, "No," and backed our man to the bed. He fell onto it, and she straddled him. "This way."

The woman took him in with a long *oooh*. "It's like you're made of electricity," she said. She began to rock slowly, smiling gravely. "I'm going to have the best kid."

Our man concentrated on how tightly her legs locked around his hips, on how protected he felt.

"You're going to be a great mom." He sighed.

She began wiggling around on top of him, tossing her hair, bucking, and it felt so good. He couldn't believe he'd been lucky enough to meet her, and at a moment when he most needed to. He watched her breasts sway, her belly heave, her mouth round into pleasure and then spread into surprise. He tucked his hands behind his head as if he were taking a nap in the park, not a care in the world, with his penis drawn inside her and about to start a family with her in just another minute or so. He was entering that buzzy state he loved, his body feeling like the glass casing of a thermometer, the liquid rising, swelling, getting dangerous—the casing could shatter!—when he thought he saw something move in the doorway; a man, a shadow, a ghost; and then it was gone.

"My kid will be the best," she chanted as she writhed.

Our man became lost in the chant. She was coming. And then he was braying, grabbing at air, coming too.

Then she quieted and stopped moving.

His climax whimpered out, replaced by a new nervousness. He cleared his throat several times, but she stayed silent and still. "Did you like that?" It was not a question our man had ever asked.

"Sure," she said, though she seemed displeased. Her smile had disappeared. She pressed her hands against his collarbones and said very somberly, "But it's not why I brought you here."

She slipped her hands around our man's throat and tightened.

Everything in him cooled. His spent limbs went wax dead. He had never been threatened by a woman before. He didn't know how to respond. Should he hit her? He couldn't.

"What's going on?" he wheezed. His rejected ejaculate gummed between them.

"Don't hate me," she said. "I'm doing this for my baby. I'm not a bad person."

"Please," our man sputtered. He struggled, but he'd been made defenseless on his back. She was strong and determined. A mother already. It all began to make sense. She *was* pregnant, had known exactly who he was, and was helping another man, the father of her child, conquer our man in order to rise in stature. She probably wasn't even from the Midwest.

Our man's sight turned to black smudges, his hearing

clotted. He groped and kicked wildly, and she held tighter. He gurgled, his chest burned. He felt so stupid. He shut his eyes and couldn't believe this was it.

How terrible life was, he marveled, but how fair. He was getting what he deserved. He thought back on how he became our man. You remember: how he'd come upon his predecessor—a man in his prime, powerful and unchallenged—copulating in the middle of Main Street, an admiring crowd gathered and traffic stopped. How our man had pummeled and bloodied him, broke his bones with his bare hands and left him to crawl a few paces away, where he died. Then how our man impregnated the woman, who was waiting and hungry, and then fourteen other women from the circle of onlookers. The crowd had never seen such a spectacle. You know the rest.

What you probably didn't know is this: It wasn't something our man had planned or ever thought he wanted. He had a girlfriend he enjoyed spending time with and fucking. She wanted to be a nurse. And he had always loved movies and thought it would be fun to do something with them. But when he'd come upon the scene—the man, the woman, the crowd—a raw yearning seized him. He felt an urgent desire to be more than he'd ever wanted to be. He gave in to this new vision: with blood on his hands he became our man. And he enjoyed it. He was proud of his work. That story of the bank tellers? He would want you to remember that he also took seven of the female customers waiting to withdraw money.

But now, what he would give to have taken a different route that day, so he wouldn't have seen that man copulating, being adored, and he wouldn't have had that feeling in his gut: That should be me.

He felt the woman's grasp let go and thought, Okay, now I'm dead, I'm released from all of this, and maybe that's a good thing. But then a hand pressed gently on his forehead, and a voice said, "Hello? Hello? Hello?"

He opened his eyes, and a woman stood over him, a different woman, one with yellow hair and wearing a nightgown. She smiled at him and lifted a baseball bat red with blood, and then he felt the sensation of something cold wrapped around his hips. He looked down to see the woman who'd attacked him, slouched to the side, rigid, her head a bloody nest of hair and bone.

The woman in the nightgown pushed the body over onto the floor and offered our man her hand. "Let's get out of here before the others track you down," she said. She pulled our man up and led him past a dead body slumped in the doorway, whose matter was sprayed along the wall. It was a man. He looked a bit like our man.

They ran through the night to another part of the city, our man barefoot and cold. Groups of young men roamed the sidewalks in search of him. They knew our man was weakened and hurt. They could smell it. They carried weapons, slapped them to their palms, jingled them if they were the jingling kind. Women lit candles in windows or on their front stoops, keeping vigil for him.

The woman was like a ghost in her nightgown, her hair blazing white under the streetlights, seemingly invisible to the others, and our man began to believe that as long as he was with her, he couldn't be seen. They crouched behind the postal boxes on corners when they saw gangs stomping toward them. They slunk behind parked cars to avoid the windows of bars where the patrons sat listening for any sound of our man. The woman cloaked him with her body to hide his scent with her own. He was aroused by her warmth. "Later," she said, touching his chest.

In the streets, sirens wailed and the city roiled, anticipating a grand change.

The woman flew through the streets, pulling our man onward.

"Just a little farther," she encouraged.

His feet were bloodied and embedded with loose asphalt, broken glass.

"Keep going," she begged.

They heard barking. A pack of dogs was gaining on the scent of the blood he spilled with each step. The woman turned into an alley and leaped to pull down a fire escape ladder. She pushed him to it. Go, go, she cried, and he climbed and she climbed after him. Above, she led the way across a mile of rooftops, still hot from the deserted sun. Pigeons startled up from their roosts and marked our man's trail through the sky for the people below to follow.

Finally, after birds, after roof jumps, zagging to a whole other city section, the din of search parties falling behind, the woman swung open a plain door and our man threw himself inside.

A room full of women sucked in their breath.

Someone whispered, "It's him." They erupted noisily like geese taking flight.

Our man saw dozens and dozens of women wringing their hands with need. He was afraid.

The woman in the nightgown led him to a chair in the middle of the room.

"You're safe here," she said. "Do you believe me?" She locked eyes with him, and he believed her.

o o o

Our man woke to a naked blonde sucking him off.

"There's a line, but I wanted to be first," she said. She roused him to his feet. They were in a windowless room with a cement floor; the twin bed he'd been sleeping on stuck out from one wall, and a small television on a metal arm from another. That was it.

The woman squeezed his hand and gazed at him, and then our man recognized her.

He pawed at her bare chest and laughed. "Where's your nightgown?" He almost wept at seeing her.

She rubbed at his face, wet-eyed, gasping. "I didn't want it to get in the way. My word, you're handsome," she said and stroked his ears, his eyes, tried to put fingers into his mouth but then stopped herself. "It's just remarkable," she said. He folded her over the bed. "Oh wow," she cried. They thrust the bed across the room.

After he came, the woman placed her hands on the floor and threw her legs up against the wall. "My doctor says this will help," she said, red-faced, her hair falling all around her, her breath strained as her insides sank toward her throat.

"You're hilarious," our man said, near to joyful tears again. He tried to do a headstand too but fell over and laughed. "I want to spend every second with you!"

She giggled. "Don't distract me!"

When she stood to leave, he asked to go with her.

"Too dangerous, babe. You stay here."

Our man asked when she would be back.

"When I can," she said, and left.

Immediately another woman walked in and began to undress.

"I'm sorry," our man said, and remembered he was naked. "You must have the wrong room."

The woman pulled a T-shirt over her head. Her tight breasts quivered. She had tattoos on her hips of terrible eagle faces. "I'm certain I don't," she said, and stepped toward him out of her skirt. She wore nothing under it.

"Oh." His mouth got wet without him being able to stop it.

"They weren't kidding," she said, running her hands up and down his chest, her fingernails leaving a tingling map that made his ears ring.

He cleared his throat. "That woman who just left. We're together." He felt ready to make a commitment, and he believed the woman in the nightgown was ready too. It would mean saying no to other women. He wanted to say no.

She tongued his ear deeply. "Is that so?"

He could feel the heat between her legs. She lowered herself slowly until she was sitting in his lap. Her muscles contracted under her skin, and our man could smell her scent mixed with a ripe perfume on her neck. She was so close and so eager, and he just couldn't help it.

A long line of women waited, and they didn't like waiting. Many were gruff and got annoyed if he asked for a minute to himself. Some were old and others far too young, so that with his arousal came a feeling of shame. Some had ailments, deformities. They were not the kind of women he usually impregnated.

It felt like weeks before the woman in the nightgown circled back to him. She seemed sad.

"I didn't think I'd need to return." She frowned. "I thought you were a sure thing."

"Didn't you want to see me?"

"Of course." She smiled thinly and patted between her legs. "Let's go. I'm ovulating."

He surprised himself—he could see he surprised her too—by weeping as he held her, as he came, and as he watched her leave. But it was different from the first time, before he knew what these captive weeks would bring, when he just felt lucky to be alive, when he thought he'd met the love of his life and he didn't think he would survive until he saw her next. He yearned only for her. But he could not convince himself she felt the same, and it left him hollow.

o o o

"Please tell me your name," our man said to the woman in the nightgown. She was curled in a ball in a corner of the mattress, as far away from him as she could be. She thought if she curled tightly enough, the baby would feel protected and so begin to grow.

"Mary," she said.

He waited for her to ask his name. When she didn't, he said, "Don't you want to know mine?"

She shrugged. "Sure."

"It's Sam."

"You don't look like a Sam."

"What do I look like?"

She peered at him. He wanted so badly to conjure a feeling of familiarity in her, a feeling like, You remind me of the past, of essences of people I once cared about, of times that might have been important to me. He wanted to be the kind of important that would make her stay. She said, "I don't know. Not Sam though."

The next time she visited him, he asked, "What do you do on the days I don't see you, Mary?"

"I work, see friends, you know."

That night he dreamed of her with her friends, and all the wonderful things they might talk about.

o o o

"Mary, can I go outside?" our man Sam asked. He'd grown pale, his shoulders had narrowed, he'd formed a paunch. "I could use a run." He crossed his arms over his stomach to hide it.

"No, you're still a wanted man." She uncrossed his arms. "Don't worry. It's what's inside that counts."

"Where have all the other women gone?" He had more free time; when the door to his room opened for another woman to enter, the waiting room looked emptier.

"They went away to have babies," Mary said sullenly.

He asked their names. He knew them only by symbols— leg scar, back tattoo, palsy. He thought knowing their names would help him imagine what their children—his children—might be like.

Mary told him: Claire, Veronica, Nan, and so on.

"What if one of them tells where I am?"

"They won't. Men are all blustery and short-sighted feelings. Women are thoughtful. We think long-term. You're good for the world."

He touched his cheeks. They were hot. He was blushing. "Am I good for you?" he asked. He felt sick in his heart.

"You better be," she said, disrobing. "You're my last hope."

But he wasn't good for her.

Maybe outside these walls he'd been replaced. Or maybe he'd managed to satisfy each woman in the city, except one. After all the other women swelled with child and left, only Mary remained, empty. And with each visit, she grew more disappointed. He didn't understand why she kept coming when all he did was fail her, but he didn't want her to stop—he would have nothing left. So he tried to try harder, though he didn't know how.

It wasn't a good life. But it was a life.

When he felt most lonely, he focused on this: He had been kept. Not cast away to be chased, battled, killed. He was being cared for by a woman who still asked him to touch her again and again, and who, at least for now, believed beyond all proof that he had something to offer. And who, in their closest moments, when our man tried to give her what she most wanted, managed to abandon some bitterness and express something like joy or pleasure or peace. It might be unconscious. It might have nothing to do with him. But he called it love. And as long as he could see it in her, he would be grateful. He would miss her when she wasn't with him, and with bile burning his throat, he would wait for her return.

THE MAST YEAR

Jane stuffed as many of her belongings into her purse as she could. She'd just been called to her boss's office and she knew what that meant. Nothing good ever came from a visit to the boss's office. If she was about to be fired, she wanted her things with her.

But in her boss's office she didn't get fired. She got a promotion. With a raise—a good one. And a bigger desk. She unpacked her things and sank into her new, better chair. She'd often thought of quitting. The job had been stagnant. The commute was long. But this made it easy to stay. That day, she even enjoyed her drive home. The traffic seemed thinner and no one honked at her.

Then, that weekend, Greg returned from a business trip with a bulge in his pocket that turned out to be a ring box. Jane watched him slide the ring onto her finger. She thought about how, when Greg moved in, his things would mix with her things until they forgot who owned what. And there would be other perks of stability, like knowing what to expect and what was expected of her. She twirled the ring, enjoying its glimmer. It was as if the world had heard what she wanted and had finally decided to deliver.

This was how her year began. And shortly after, the first people arrived.

One morning, Jane found a man and woman sleeping in each other's arms near her roses. Jane figured they were homeless, though they didn't have that scruffy look. Perhaps they were drunk and had gotten lost. Their presence unnerved her, but she told herself they would leave in a day or so, and what was the harm?

The next day two tents stood under her willow. A few children ran around, and a man with a long beard moved landscaping stones into a circle.

During the night, Jane's sleep was disturbed by hammering. She woke to a crowd of men, women, and children huddled under umbrellas, tents, and tarps strung between the trees. There looked to be at least forty people. When Jane peered out the front door, they cheered.

She called her mother.

"Sounds like a mast year," her mother said. Jane heard a game show in the background.

"You mean this is a thing?"

"Yes, it's a thing. It's a thing that happens to trees. But sometimes it happens to people too."

Her mother explained that some years trees grew far more nuts than in ordinary years. A year of abundance was called a mast year. Somehow, as if the trees were calling to them, animals from all over sensed the tree's prodigious bounty and swarmed it. They gorged. "I'll send you a book about it. It's short. More like a pamphlet."

"But I'm not a tree."

"You're like a tree. You drink water. You're tall. You're sweet."

"Mom."

"Jane. When people have mast years it's because they're having extra good fortune. Like you with your raise and engagement. Don't you think you're very fortunate right now?"

"Things are going well, but—"

"People want to join in your good fortune. So let them. You said to the world, 'I've got something you want.' You shook your limbs and said, 'Come.' So they came."

"Sorry, Mom, but I didn't 'shake my limbs.' I didn't *do* anything."

"Well, *sorry*, honey, but you did. They wouldn't be here otherwise."

"Mom." Jane sighed. She wished she hadn't called.

"Jane, relax. You'll love it. You'll be surrounded by people who think you're wonderful. *Because you are.* They'll feel lucky. And you'll feel like a saint when it's over. It's only a year. What's one year?"

o o o

Jane wanted to tell Greg herself, but he'd already found out from work friends. He made a big show of ringing her bell and presenting her with flowers at the door even though he had a key and could have just come inside. Jane blushed and tried to usher him in, but he caught her around the waist and dipped her into a movie-style kiss. The crowd clapped their hands. Someone yelled, "Woo!"

Greg called out, "This woman loves *me*." He puffed his chest.

But once inside, Greg slumped. "Why are you doing this?" he whined.

"It's just a thing that's happening," she said.

"Well, make it stop."

"I can't. I don't know how."

"That's not what I heard."

"Excuse me?"

"Aren't I paying enough attention to you?"

"Yes, you're fine. We're fine."

"Then make them go away. They're going to think I don't do enough for you."

"But you do."

"Then why are they here?"

"I don't know." She kissed his neck. "Maybe I'm not doing enough for *you*."

o o o

Jane tried to wake early so she could bring Greg breakfast in bed, but he was already in the kitchen when she came down. On the table was Greg's signature omelet, cut in two and plated, and mugs of coffee, hers fixed how she liked it.

"I also made a coffee cake, but it isn't ready yet," he said. His brow seemed to frown.

"You make coffee cake?" She smelled vanilla and something bitter.

He glanced quickly out the window. "I *always* make coffee cake," he said, sounding hurt. The crowd looked hungry.

"Well, great," she said, settling into a chair, "I love coffee cake," even though she thought it was just okay. "Is it your signature coffee cake?" she asked, looking at her beige omelet.

"Why, yes. It is." He laughed with relief, glancing out the window again. "You're lucky. I'm a man with a signature everything." His half of the omelet was gone, and he stood to go. He kissed her roughly, as though marking his territory. But then his kiss turned tender, and she blushed. The faces in the window were smeared with achy smiles.

"Be a doll and take that out in five," Greg said, took two twenties from her wallet, and left.

She dumped the rest of her omelet into the trash. It was nice that he had signature things, but really *signature* just meant *one*, and his signature omelet wasn't very good. She tasted a corner of the coffee cake. It was salty. Jane cut it into pieces and arranged them on a platter. She would tell him she couldn't stop eating it.

As she pulled out of the garage, people gathered to touch her car. She triggered the door locks. Their clothing wiped the windows. Metal jacket buttons pinged the car like rain. Their faces showed deep concentration, as if they were placing a smell that had once been familiar. They held small trinkets in their hands, wood and stone talismans, stacked brownies tied with ribbons. They offered these to her.

"No," she said from behind the glass. "You keep those. I don't need them. Don't *you* need them?" The brownies looked good. Her mouth watered. But no, this was what it was all about. They were in need and she could give, and then they would leave, right? She inched the window down enough to slip them the plated coffee cake. Someone in a wool hunter's coat took it. "Sorry, it's not very good," she explained through the crack. "I didn't make it. I will next time. I promise."

They sniffed the cake and put crumbs to their tongues, tentative, she assumed, because she had claimed not to like it. She knocked on the window.

"Go ahead. It's good, it's fine," she urged. They began to stuff chunks into their mouths. Their faces gave away that, truly, it wasn't good at all. She thought they might spit it out and leave, decide that if her first offering was crappy coffee cake, it wasn't worth the hassle. But they continued to eat it.

○ ○ ○

The news crews came. She saw her house on television. She saw herself, pretaped, standing at her kitchen window, lit bright against the darkening evening, washing dishes, her hair electric on one side and matted on the other. Onscreen, she was wearing Greg's college track T-shirt, and she remembered it as the day they'd both called in sick just for fun.

Watching it, she unconsciously smoothed down her hair.

After the news broadcast, people bloomed like mold across her yard, over where she'd planned to put a pool, threading through the forest border of the property. People climbed trees and built houses in them. She watched whole families disappear into the branches in the evening, then climb down each morning to pick through her garbage.

When the lawn and trees filled, people burrowed underground. They fought each other for shelter. When a man came up from his burrow, he cautiously looked around. Occasionally someone was waiting there to bash his head, drag his limp body from the hole, and then scurry in. The victim would eventually come to and crawl away, embarrassed that even here his luck had run out.

Wires fanned out from Jane's hacked electric and cable up into the trees and down all the holes, like streams off a mountain.

Jane had to bake for hours each morning. She bagged lunches for those who worked, passed out milk money to children lined up for the caravan of rerouted school buses, held babies so their mothers could get a shower in at the portable facilities Jane had rented. The people, like devotees, lined up before her, and Jane caressed each of their cheeks to give them strength for the day ahead. Then she drove to work. She was disappointed when her boss suggested she begin working from home—productivity was down due to everyone wanting to stand around her. She liked her new job. Even more, she liked going to work and leaving her house behind.

o o o

"There were twelve birthdays that needed cakes today. And somehow they've got me tutoring all the fourth-graders. Can this not take too long?"

"Don't you think this is fun?" Greg said, smiling with all his teeth. "*I* think it's fun."

"No, you don't." Jane wouldn't use the word *fun*. She didn't think it was anything but exhausting to feel responsible for so many people.

Usually they peeled their clothes off in bed according to which body part they were trying to locate. But now Greg undressed slowly in front of the window. "Come over here. I'd like to make you come over here." Lately, he'd made a show of really enjoying it.

"No. The bed is a fine place for that."

They fought over lights on or lights off, and she won, but even in the dark she could tell when he peered out the window and flexed.

"It's so much better now," he insisted loudly, rolling her into a different position. "Don't you agree? I think I'm a better lover now. Don't you think I've become a better lover?"

"You're the same," she said. She hadn't meant to sound unencouraging. He was going through a sensitive time. She tried to apologize by moaning loudly.

He lapped at her closest body part—her elbow—making a face like he was in a foreign country, eating gross food his host family presented him. An *I love it* behind a false grin. She didn't like it either.

She situated herself on top of him, tried to pull a blanket over her shoulders, but Greg tore it off. She placed his hands over her breasts so anyone watching couldn't see them bounce. "Nothing is different," she whispered. "And that's good."

"Oh no," he said. Then again, "No," and she thought he disagreed. Then he said, "Yes," like he'd reconsidered. And then again, "Yes." Then he came with theatrical force, almost bucking her off him. "Wasn't that incredible?" he panted. "Wasn't it incredible for you?" He acted more in love with her than ever, and so it felt like much less.

"It was great."

"Let's go again. I'll do better."

But Jane climbed off.

Greg's face drooped. "Please," he whimpered and gripped her.

Jane sensed the stillness of all the people outside, listening to them. The crickets were silent, as though listening too.

○ ○ ○

Her mother sent a thin, dog-eared paperback called *My Mast Year*. It had large print and clearly was self-published. On the cover the author, Penny Smith, contemplated something soft in the distance; her eyes sparkled with spotlight diamonds while a chain of real diamonds squeezed her neck.

Inside were gauzy photos of Penny baking pies, Penny reading to children by her fireplace, Penny cooking a shiny goose for what looked like thousands of people crowding her ornate dining room. In picture after picture, people lounged over her furniture, leafed through her books, slept in her beds. They gazed at her with an aggressive love.

Jane had been generous, but she hadn't been welcoming or gracious. She should think of this as an extended dinner party where everyone drinks too much and has to stay over. They should feel at home and be glad to be there. And in the sobering daylight, they would feel rested and satiated enough to leave.

She went to her front door, unlocked it, threw it open, and went to bed.

○ ○ ○

At first, they were skittish; they hid as though they didn't believe her invitation had been genuine. But she'd catch clues that they'd been there during the night. Dirty mugs in the sink. New shows recorded on the DVR.

When Jane entered a room, a sense of movement lingered in the air. As if a minute before, the room had been filled with people who'd hid at the sound of her. She felt on the verge of a surprise party every time she turned on the lights.

At night, she yawned loudly and said, "I'm going to bed," into the seemingly empty rooms. The house creaked to life once her light went out.

One morning, she came downstairs to find a few people sitting around her kitchen table, digging into a pie she'd made the day before. At the sight of her, they tensed, but they didn't run. They lifted their forks to her and said, "Good pie."

Jane nodded. "Thank you."

From then on, people occupied every room. Late into the evenings they huddled in earnest conversation along every wall, lounged on furniture, on the floor, slept under and on the dining room table. Their laughter drowned out her music, the radio news she liked to listen to. She believed they must be getting what they needed, and that she had helped them get it. But her house was now very crowded. The dishes were always dirty. There was never a chair to sit on. The shower drains were clogged with hair. She couldn't do any housecleaning without being jostled. And no one helped. Each morning she had to shoo people out of the laundry room, where the couples falling in love would go to be alone. She restocked toilet paper several times a day. She only found solace in her bedroom. She'd tacked a note on the door asking for privacy, which, thankfully, they respected.

o o o

On date night, Greg wrestled everyone out of the kitchen. "Come back later," he said. "We're trying to have a romantic dinner because we're so in love." The crowd regrouped in the kitchen doorway. Some of them threw pennies at him, which had become an insult in the house. Jane worried that people didn't like him. It made her self-conscious.

"You have to be nicer," she warned.

"I'm nice." He picked up a penny that had landed in his lap and chucked it back. The crowd booed.

Jane laid a seared steak in front of him, yawning.

"You should sleep," he said.

She rolled her eyes. "There's no time."

They ate. When Greg had finished his steak, Jane passed him the rest of hers. "Why don't you give that to them?" He was trying to be nicer.

She imagined them setting upon the meat like dogs, turning over lamps and tables, hurting each other. She would have to dress their wounds all evening. "No, there's not enough."

Just then a man sauntered into the kitchen. Like he owns the place, Jane thought, flushing with anger. She recognized him. He had a tent by her mailbox and went through her mail. She'd bought a shredder because of him. But she noticed the crowd of people in the doorway winking at her. A few gave her a thumbs-up sign, and she realized they liked this man.

"You gonna eat that?" the man drawled, pointing to the chunk of steak that sat between Jane and Greg.

"Who do you think you are?" Jane asked. She made her voice hostile, but really she wanted to know.

There was something rogue about him. Like he would be a bad addition to anyone's life. But his eyes were saggy and kind, like a dog's. He extended a hand. "I'm West."

"That's not your name," she said, crossing her arms.

"No, but I wish it was." He smiled then, and she could make out deep dimples hidden beneath his disorganized beard. The discovery made her blush.

Greg stood. "Excuse me. This is a private dinner."

West breathed deep. "And what a delicious private dinner it is," he said, and winked at Jane. "Why don't you share?"

"I am sharing," she said.

"Are you though?"

What did he mean *share*? She felt like a victim of sharing. She'd tripled her grocery budget and had given in to the requests for sugar cereal. She'd instituted nightly storytelling around the bonfire for the children. As she spoke, those at her feet tied and untied her shoelaces or drew vines around her ankles. They stayed up past their bedtime because their parents took too many sips from the whiskey flasks they'd insisted she provide. The parents tottered around the yard flashing her tipsy grins. But other times she knew she'd displeased them. She'd taken on Greg's student loans in anticipation of their wedding. She'd heard grumbling that it meant less for everyone else. Is that what West was saying? Was she expected to pay off everyone's loans?

She pulled the plate to her and methodically sectioned

the meat. Greg said, "Honey," in protest, but West put up his hand and Greg quieted.

She chewed and swallowed each piece. She *mmm*ed like she loved every bite, though she thought she might be sick. West watched her mouth do this work, and then he smirked and winked again.

Later in bed, Greg pouted. "Why did you eat the steak?"

The steak still felt lodged in her stomach. Like she'd eaten a golf ball. "You didn't want it."

"But you *gave* it to me." Greg rolled over and clicked the light off. "You gave it to *me*."

o o o

When Jane found herself in the same room as West, people winked and made kissing noises. Notes were passed to her at the kitchen table. *West likes you.*

"But I love Greg," she would say.

They would shrug. "But don't you like West?"

She did like West. She couldn't look at West without imagining his tongue on her skin. She wondered if he was a doting or selfish lover. She wanted him to be selfish. She thought from his smirk he might be, and she liked the idea of something that required no compromises, no special kindness, no giving. Just taking. She found the stuff of love hard to juggle with all the other stuff like cooking, cleaning, yard work. When Greg left for a week-long business trip, she felt relief for many reasons.

West became a fixture inside the house then, where there was so much more to be gotten than mail. He played music in the evenings, thumping out songs he'd written on the piano. Secretly, Jane liked to watch him play these songs, and at times she suspected that he played them for her. One must have been for her, because at the chorus West sang her name over and over again. The tune drifted into the kitchen, where she was sandwiched between two knitters, their needles and elbows jabbing her with each stitch. She could see West's back when he leaned in and out of the piano emotionally. The parlor was full of people, and they all laughed behind their hands and said, "Aww," like they'd just seen a baby. When West finished, everyone was quiet. From the ridge high above the house she heard the hollow echo of gunshots. Some night hunting. Or someone else's mast year gone wrong, perhaps.

Jane climbed the stairs to her bedroom, and they all watched her. She slid into bed and flicked off the light. A moment later West arrived and slid in beside her. She invited him to do what he wanted. She felt used and generous all at once. After, she asked if that was what he'd meant by sharing.

West moved in permanently. He brought nothing with him. As a first act, he moved Greg's things to the front lawn where they were picked through by the crowd and eventually by a weepy Greg. West dealt with the mail, paid the bills, answered correspondence. Jane hadn't expected him to be helpful, but he was. He let Greg's loan payments default. She knew it was happening but pretended not to.

Inside the house, people patted her on the back.

"We never liked him," they said of Greg. "He was so needy. He tried too hard."

Jane didn't bother to explain that he hadn't always been like that. He'd been fun; it had been nice, easy.

Her mother welcomed the news. She too had never liked him.

"If he was so awful," Jane asked, "why did all these people come?" Now that her engagement was off, would they leave? That had been her hope.

"Oh honey, there's more to you than some boy and some job. Maybe there's a secret in you. Maybe there's something in you that's about to burst."

Jane liked this idea.

o o o

Jane hadn't thought she wanted much from West. But he was steady and calm and she found herself relying on him more and more. As her feelings for him grew, so did the crowds. They doubled, then tripled. The old house shuddered under the weight. Parties went on all night. Sometimes into the mornings. The cushions of Jane's couch were deflated, all her curios had disappeared from her curio cabinet, all her books from her bookshelves. People drank and accused one another of slights. Fights broke out regularly now. People got injured. Ambulances came. The sirens screamed up and down her street, a seemingly endless loop of extreme alarm.

At night, Jane and West whispered under bedsheets so no one could hear.

"What made you come and live by my mailbox?" Jane asked him once.

"I just had a feeling I should."

"I'm glad you did." She felt him smile in the darkness.

West always fell asleep first, while Jane remained awake, holding him or holding his hand, listening to the night commotion in her house. All Jane wanted was to eat a nice, quiet dinner with West, to get to know him better without so many bodies pressing into them, living their love vicariously. But that possibility seemed farther away than ever.

o o o

On movie night, Jane and West couldn't find an empty spot on the couch. The floor was covered, head to toe. They stood in the corner and balanced their beers and popcorn. People grabbed fistfuls from their bowl until the popcorn was gone. They wiped their buttery hands on Jane's pants.

A large plaid-clad man was controlling the remote. A home renovation show was on.

West tried pulling rank. "It's movie night."

The large man said, "It's *Ace the Wrecker* marathon night."

Others called out the news, trivia, or crime shows they wanted to watch.

West contested. "But I signed up for this time. It's movie night."

Everyone turned to Jane for a final verdict. "Leave me out of this," she snapped.

The large man catcalled, "You could use help around here. I can build an addition in exchange for a little—" He made a lewd gesture.

Jane dropped West's hand and pushed through the crowd. The people pushed back. She stepped over heads and the hands that reached for her, groped at her ankle, her knee. They tried to reach higher. They pulled at her sweater, clutched at her belt. Arms looped around her waist. Her hair was yanked. She scratched her way out.

When she slipped into bed, she found four children hiding under the comforter, a rumple she thought was just bunched sheets. The children clung to her and called her Mommy. She could not free herself, so she lay limp while they mewled. West arrived and peeled the children from her and scooted them out the door.

When she and West made love that night, she saw shadowy figures hovering in the doorway. As she tried to sleep, she felt their breath on her through the sheets.

All night, the house stairs creaked; people thudded down hallways, in and out of rooms, slamming doors, laughing, yelling, fighting. Music blared, people fucked, moaned, glass broke. Jane shook. West held her and smoothed her hair.

"Hang in there, kiddo," he said. "It's only July."

She turned from him and wept.

∘ ∘ ∘

Jane woke alone. She smelled bacon and knew West had cooked for her. He was always doing small, thoughtful things.

He sat at her kitchen table, but so did forty others. They left no place for her. People perched along the counters, their heels banging against her cupboards. All the burners burned, the microwave buzzed, the oven was on broil. Something even cooked over a fire in her fireplace.

West looked up at Jane from the newspaper, ratty and worn as if it had already been read a hundred times that morning. Two plates of breakfast sat in front of him. He had waited, and seeing her then, picked up a strip of bacon and held it under his nose like a mustache, even though he had a full beard. Desire thrummed in her, and she said, "You're so cute," but it was drowned out by all the morning noise. He smiled, but she knew he hadn't heard her.

Shouting began over by the toaster. More voices joined. Something about cinnamon toast. A scuffle erupted. People surged to escape the fight and both of Jane's feet left the floor as she was pressed upward by the bodies around her. She screamed. The nearest people shrank from her and let her fall to her knees.

She had lost sight of West. She heard him call out, his voice filled with concern but far away. "Are you okay?"

Jane couldn't speak. She punched her way through the crowd, wanting to harm, and once inside her bedroom, slid all the furniture in front of the door, even the wicker hamper which held only one sock. Someone had stolen all her dirty clothes.

By midday, West was able to force himself into the bedroom. Jane sat stiffly in bed. He approached with caution, as if she was either delicate or dangerous. He tried to hold her.

"Don't touch me," she said coldly.

His eyes widened. "Why not?" He tried to hold her again.

"I don't want people touching me."

"But it's me," he said, his voice soft with confusion. "I'm different."

He was different. That was the problem. "You need to go," she said.

"But I can help. Let me help you."

"Help? You can't help me. I don't even love you."

"That's not true," he said, not believing it.

"Yes, it is," she said, through tears now. "Get out."

"You do too love me. I can see it." He tried to sound certain, but he shook his head, stunned.

"You're wrong. This whole world was wrong. I have nothing to give you. So leave."

"Honey, you don't really believe that. That's not what you want."

"You have no idea what I want."

"So tell me."

But she didn't know what to say. She felt a strong desire to be alone, but she didn't know how long that feeling would last. And she didn't equate that desire with knowing what she really wanted. She said nothing.

West smoothed her cheeks, but he failed to find her behind hardened eyes, and so he reluctantly packed a bag, a bag he hadn't arrived with, full of things that didn't belong to him, and left.

News spread through the house, out to the yards, up the trees and underground. Conversations died in the living room. People quickly got out of Jane's way when they saw her coming. For the first time in what felt like years, she went a full day without brushing shoulders with someone.

When the food ran out, she didn't buy more. People scrounged in the garbage, hunted for scraps in the yard. The hunger set in. Motley caravans began to leave, clanging down the streets at all hours. People insisted Jane buy supplies to make them snacks and bagged lunches for the road, pay their bus fare, drive them to the airport. "You owe us," they said, but she gave them nothing. They threw pennies at her, then collected what fell at her feet. They would need them.

"Mom, they're leaving."

"What did you do?"

"I kicked West out."

"Oh honey, why?"

"I don't know. They steal my stuff."

"You have plenty of stuff."

"It was too much. I couldn't take it."

"How am I not surprised? You have no follow-through. You never have."

"Mom."

"Jane. What's one year? You were happy. They were happy."

"I wasn't happy."

"Well, is this what you wanted?" her mother said. "Now who's happy?"

∘ ∘ ∘

Jane found a naked woman slumped in the shower. The woman was slack-jawed in the relentless spray, her pouty mouth like a cherubic water feature spouting water down her chin, her breasts. Jane pulled her onto the bathroom tile, where she lay splayed for days, barely breathing. Eventually the woman dragged herself down the stairs, trailing rust-colored urine. Jane listened to the drag all night.

The last people crawled away on their hands and knees, stricken by the sudden lack. Their eyes were yellowed, their skin blotchy. Behind the couch, Jane found two corpses, their gray, confused faces covered by a sheet. She recognized them. A new couple. A thing started here.

They'd stayed too long, perhaps believing her fortunes would change.

She dragged these leaden bodies to one of the empty burrows and dropped them in. They hit like apples hit the floor.

The burrows in the yard sank with no families to keep them from caving. The tree-house nails rusted, and wind worried some boards from the branches. At night, Jane heard the creak of swinging pieces. Her house groaned above the shifting ground, and the floors settled into new, unnerving contours. The nighttime glowed green against her windows, and her room felt full of muck.

She was alone. She hadn't meant to be this alone.

This is how her year ended: Occasionally someone would show up, most often some man down on his luck, having heard about a woman with prodigious good fortune to share. She would welcome him, buy him things, cook and serve his meals, take him in her bed or anywhere he wanted and he would find it all soothing. The man would be hopeful that his life was changing. But eventually he would realize no good could be found in such a desolate-feeling house. The man would stay a week more, eating her cooking, sleeping with her, because she made it easy to.

But then Jane would wake alone. She'd search, hoping to surprise the man in a dark closet, under a bed, all the places where she used to find people without even trying. But Jane would only ever find something missing. A box of her grandmother's jewelry. Her checkbook. Stereo equipment.

She kept a log of all the things that had been taken from her that year. It sat heavily on her kitchen table. On mornings she'd sit before it, the sunrise making the wood table glimmer like the surface of a pond, slightly quaking from her unsteady breath and anxious knees, the wood grain arcing longways like bug trails on the water. She'd wait, peering down the road and drumming her fingernails on the table, the dense sound ricocheting around the house, into all the empty rooms, finally settling like leaves in her lap.

THE NOT-
NEEDED FOREST

I get told I am Not Needed by a man in a suit. This only happens to ten-year-old boys, and only some. My mother cries and cries on the suit, and the man's face budges not a bit. He says simply, as she is sobby, Ma'am, would you like the State to make a status exception for just your boy?

Of course, I know this trick from school, but Ma makes grateful saucer eyes and wiggles. Oh, would you?

So I hold her arm to steady her because it's clear she isn't ready for his two-punch.

There are no exceptions from the State.

o o o

The next day I put my belongings on the curb, and the Needed boys come for the good toys—my bike, skates, mitt—the things any ten-year-old wants; their mothers search for the clothes that fit and are warm, shoes of the right size. My pile is not the only one on the block.

Birds smother the trees, and to pass the time we throw rocks at them, hover while they sit stunned and blinking on the ground. We don't mess with them there. Once they rise back up to the branches, we try to hit them again. I stun the same bird three times, which cheers me. It's a hard game, but I'm good at it.

At dinner my father swirls his brown drink, looks at my mother with this expression I don't know. Maybe he can't settle on a feeling. He shrugs as if to say something.

My mother throws a spoon at him, yells. I know *her* look.

Ma, I cry. It's no one's fault.

My father's face crumples.

I say, It's random.

Ma says, Oh random, my eye.

I've never seen her so ugly.

o o o

In the morning, I board the bus. It's a solemn ride. We look out the windows at our city disappearing. People on their way to work, girls in pretty dresses lined up outside a school. We hear the hollow *huts* of boys playing football. Boys we'll never be. Then we're speeding by dumps, by corn and cows and silos, reservoirs and fields of tree stumps, new swamps. We drive for hours, and many of us fall asleep.

We jolt awake at the Processing Hub, dead center in a mud lot of buses coughing darkness, buses full of boys like us.

I'm draped in a thin paper smock. My shoes are taken. I wait for hours that seem even longer in a line that coils and squeezes itself as we jostle for some last breathing room. Boy after boy, stoic or weepy, slides into the Chute. Here, the Chute is just a hole that makes a sucking noise. But beyond, it's a long, snaking tube that leads to the Incineration Center. It's a means to an end.

At the front of the line, a white-coated processor sits at a cluttered desk, his hair flying up, sucked by the Chute. He holds a clipboard of bulging paper, and when I tell him my name, he rustles through the pages and jots the time in a column, ENTERED CHUTE.

The processor says, Please get in the Chute.

I remind myself that this is my status, this is just the way things are. I tell myself, *You had a nice time*; even, *Maybe it's better this way*. I allow one last, fun, deep, muscle-straining breath, the kind you take before you dive into the quarry—the breath of being most alive—and I slide into the Chute.

o o o

I tumble toward the roar and rising heat of the Incinerator, trying not to think of life things, which only makes me think of them more. It's an unfair game. The walls turn pocked and buckled. They are warming. Just as I'm trying not to think of Ma baking cookies, I wrap hard into a curve and bang against the side and stop. I hear a suck and a pop behind me; another boy has entered the Chute. I try to pull myself forward, to squeak my own way to my death. But I'm stuck. I feel cool air tickle my leg, and I realize my foot is no longer in the Chute. I feel around with my hands. I'm able to slip fingers out, then my arm. More cool air rushes at my face from where my arm and foot are. I'm caught in a hole; a fissure in the seam of the Chute. My stomach flutters. Around the curve, the funneling wind picks up, tugs at my body. I can hear the next boy hurtling toward me as I scrape my other leg through the hole, then the rest of me. I barely think about what I'm doing—that I'm going against my fate, the State, my status—and the consequences of it. I just have this feeling inside, like, *Win*.

And then I'm cold and in a stinking, mushy pit below the Chute, and it's hollow dark. A pair of eyes blinks white at me, and I hear, Shush. Lots of teeth are smiling. A boy's voice whispers, Can you believe it? And we find hands in the dark and squeeze, ecstatic. We *can't* believe it.

We escaped the Chute! We're not dead!

We wait in mud until the whirring Chute quiets. The end of Processing. It's even harder to see our teeth and eyes now, as if the night has gotten deeper. We move toward the sound of frogs, and steadily we are more boys. We slither under a fence and through dark grass, run for an even darker line: a forest.

We bushwhack, try to navigate by stars, follow a river, eat what we find: little berries and thwacked oily nuts. We sing songs we'd sung in school. We tell jokes. As our eyes adjust, we throw rocks at skulking animals. A squirrel dies. We realize how hungry we are. We peel its skin, eat it raw. We puke.

The sun climbs, and a boy starts shouting, This way! A camp! I've found a camp!

He runs ahead and we run after, along the sandy and

mucky river edge, until we break through the trees and into a clearing.

Black stones ring a pile of flaky, charred wood. A rough structure hides beneath a blanket of evergreen branches.

We mill about, touching things—animal bones, hatches in a tree to mark the passing days. A black soup pot and a ladle, a sharp blade, deer hides tacked up to dry.

The boy who found the camp holds up a stick, shrieking, This is an arrow!

We huddle, look nervously to the tangled trees surrounding us. We see that fourteen of us escaped the Chute. Fourteen boys, naked and shimmering with mud.

We should have buddies, one boy says. We think this is a good idea and pair off. I am with a boy named George. The two Michaels are together, and so we name the scrawny one Small Michael. Carl is the tallest, and he pairs with Alfred, the boy who found the camp, who is almost as tall. He is muscular too, in a way none of the other boys are muscular. Because they are tall and strong, they easily seem like the leaders. Ryan and Brian are paired, Joe and Davey, Fred and Frank, Steven and Gil.

Small Michael asks, What is this place? He sounds spooked, like a girl.

Must be an abandoned hunting camp, Alfred says. It must be very old.

Do you think we're the first boys to escape the Chute? Carl asks.

We can't be, I say, thinking of that hole that grabbed my leg and jerked me to a stop.

We must be, Alfred says. Otherwise there would be a whole community here of boys like us. But older.

It makes sense. Where would such boys have gone? Not-Neededs are not welcome anywhere.

This is when we understand that we're here for good. We get quiet.

What are you whittling? Carl asks Alfred.

The arrow, Alfred says, and he holds it up. The point is dull. I'm making it pointier.

The point is now very pointy. He throws it at a tree, and it sinks in deep. He laughs. Alfred has a small laugh.

There's no bow, he says, but I'll just throw it and hit something meaty. How hard can it be?

Alfred disappears into the woods, and before the pot of water is boiling he returns with a deer, small like a fawn but past its spots. He cleans, skins and hunks it, and we skewer the meat on broken saplings, roast it over a popping fire.

When we are full and warm and lying around the fire, drifting, I say, We are charmed boys.

The others sleepily hoorah, and Alfred smiles at me through the flickery orange light.

L ife with boys is great!

No one tells us to behave, and yet we do. In our own way. When we get that feeling in our pits, we go into the woods and wrench large branches from living trees. We can pummel the flank of a dead deer and scream, and we don't have to answer why because no one is asking us why.

We all know why. We're boys. We'll stun a bird and twist its neck, and we're on to the next thing. We don't ask what did it ever do to us. We'll set fires and watch them burn, and later, when we feel better, we'll put them out. And wouldn't you know, those fire spots bloom mushrooms for us to eat.

We get good at foraging. We have nut piles and traps to catch the squirrels that raid them. We collect bird eggs, and we eat the mom. A few boys become ace whittlers, and to shoot their arrows we bend bows from saplings, thread them with stretched sinew. We have a nice, organized camp, and when we yearn for our mothers, we have each other. No boy gives another boy a hard time ever.

The height of summer means berries. The small trees grow taller, and we hide among them when we hunt. We play games. Some old games, but also some new ones with extra-fun parts. Davey made up a tug-of-war done in heats. Ryan made up a chase through the forest, with tagging and spotting and no feet touching the ground. Everyone has a game, and we play them all, and no one has a favorite.

Each game has rules, and we make them complicated. That's where our mothers got us wrong—boys like rules. But rules must also be a kind of game.

Sometime in late summer Alfred builds an obstacle course. It goes like this: Wade through the mud pit, swim across the river to the maze he hacked into grasses that have sprung human height along the banks. Out of the maze, slide under the fence of thorny branches he's woven, and race to touch the deer-pelted tree. At that point the rules end. If you are fast, you can run to win. If you are strong, you can tackle the runner. If you are clever, you can let someone strong tackle someone fast, and while they wrestle, you win.

The first day we race the course, we finish ecstatic and spent under the tree.

When'd you do all this? we wheeze.

Alfred says, Sometimes I can't sleep.

o o o

The leaves turn and fall, and we know we're near winter. We crudely stitch skins together for warmth. Mushrooms explode; we fight animals for nuts. The deer huff down leaves like vacuums. All the animals we see are stuffing their faces, but many more have disappeared, getting tight in their dens. All the delicious berries are gone. Brian found an apple tree deep in the forest and picked every last one. We make ourselves sick on apples, then bury the rest in a hole for storage. Alfred says the tree is a sign there once was a farm here.

One morning we wake nestled in snow. The fire has been doused by melt. It smokes and sizzles. We shake the clumps off our sleeping pelts and sit in silence. We've only ever known winter in our homes.

We are months past our scheduled deaths, and now we are nearly starved.

We've eaten our nuts, our apples, our seeds, our mushrooms, our dried deer and squirrel and rabbit and fish. We break water from the frozen river. We suck on bark, chew leaves that have already been chewed by worms. We hook fingers around bones we never knew we had. This is our new game because we're too tired to run.

We dig through the snow for animal bones to boil. We must have squandered something when we were just new and careless boys, left scraps decomposing on the forest floor. We roam deeper and deeper into the woods, days from our camp, sleep in the open so that we can travel even farther. One day we see a track and follow it up into the mountains, where we find a deer struggling in the snow and pounce, kill it with our hands even though we have weapons. We just don't think. But it's a starved deer, almost meatless, and it gives us strength for only a week. Every creature is a ghost. We can't find the end of the forest to leave it, and we can't leave it because we have nowhere to go.

o o o

Davey is curled around a tree, his neck turned like he's looking at something in the middle of his back. He is dead.

Maybe he was climbing and fell.

Maybe he was chasing an animal and didn't see the tree.

Who cares what happened, Alfred says. What are we going to do with him?

We stand around the body, kick holes in the crusty snow.

A few boys punch their guts guiltily. Their stomachs are cursing.

George says, Don't do that. Don't even think it.

Michael says, But he *is* dead.

George says, Can't we just say congratulations, we beat the Chute? We did our best out here, but it got too hard?

And just let death come without a fight? cries Brian.

A boo rises in my throat, but I stuff it back down.

Alfred says, Survivors always say yes.

But we *have* survived, George practically whispers, his eyes on Davey's gaping mouth, his slack, black tongue. We're not even supposed to be alive.

If we don't, I say shakily, some animal will. What's the difference?

Some boys nod at me, and I'm proud, then embarrassed.

We drag Davey back to camp, but George stays in the woods. It's a good day for walking, he says. The sun is shining.

The meal is not delicious, though that seems appropriate for poor Davey. We are full, and we don't feel better.

What's left of him we smoke, string up the meat in trees to keep. We gather his bones—we'll boil them in a desperate broth. We ball the bloodied snow to suck on later. All the while, we clutch our stomachs and weep. After starvation this sudden food brings great pain.

George returns in the moonlight. I spy him taking tentative bites off scraps as the others sleep.

o o o

After a week Davey is gone, and we're hungry boys again.

What are we to do? we say gravely. We eye one another and wish someone would keel over and die.

Alfred replies, equally gravely, As many as can, must survive in order to keep this place going, for all the Not-Needed boys to come.

We nod. We hope we all survive.

He says, It's wrong, what the State did to us. Doesn't each boy deserve a chance to earn his own life? Alfred is standing on a boulder. He looks very official.

We nod again, some of us more vehemently than others. I'm reminded of my mother and her last bitter face.

Please, Alfred, George says. Please don't say what you're about to say. He doesn't have to *say* it, though. We all *know*.

Alfred steps down from the boulder and wanders among us. He touches our shoulders. They are bones. As many as can, *must* survive, he repeats. Our lives are valuable, aren't they? We should be given a chance to *earn* them. He makes a fist. We should earn our lives through competition. The loser hasn't earned his right to live, but in losing he gives the rest of us another chance. He pauses. And in turn we give the loser what the State couldn't—a fair death. What boy can hope for more? It's the only right thing.

He returns to his rocky perch. Let's fight for our lives like we're meant to. Let's show the State what it means to be fair and just.

All the boys nod. We feel hungry. We feel horrible. We want to feel anything else. So we close our eyes and cast sticks. Alfred counts. We have all agreed it is right. Even George.

o o o

We decide on a race through the woods, and mark the route with bones hung from trees. It is deemed a fair course because sometimes it's hard for tall boys, and other times for short. There are log piles to climb over, so speed alone won't win, and confusing turns to navigate, and false paths, so cleverness helps.

We gather at the start, shake and stretch our arms, legs. We are very nervous, and some boys cry. Not me, though. I'm a forager, and I know the forest well. Carl looks quick and primed, like a match just getting lit. Alfred seems bored.

He calls us to the line, and we're off.

I reach the end first, with Carl close behind. The rest of the boys stagger in. Small Michael is last. He's bitterly disappointed, and in a way so are we. He's very small, and there are so many of us.

We carry him back to the camp and throw him a party as the sun slides behind the cold horizon. We weave him a crown from dry river grass, pretty it with evergreen. We tell his stories, like how the first time he arrowed a deer, he laughed so hard he trickled pee. We overmarvel at his knowledge of star names, at his singing voice. We ask him to sing one more of his midnight songs.

But he shakes his head. Staring into the fire, he hands Alfred the large stone. We agreed that this would be the signal, and that once the stone is in play, no one can object.

If possible, Small Michael says quietly, tell my mother I didn't die in the Chute. I killed a bear for you all and suffered mortal wounds. He tilts back his head.

We look away as Alfred slits his throat.

∘ ∘ ∘

We play juggle ball, bone toss, tug-of-war in heats. We make new obstacles and race the course. We run, jump, crab-walk, balance on our hands. Whittling an arrow that pierces or a whistle that toots is combined with a tree-climb or race to even it out; whittling is a fine skill, but any boy can run for his life.

After each game we build a fire, weave a crown, tell stories, celebrate the boy who lost, until the stone is in play. Then we eat. We say we hope we'll never have to compete again.

A week passes, sometimes longer. Then we decide on the next game. We vote, and everyone has to agree. It can take a few rounds, some arguing, before we are ready to play. Fred, Frank, Steven, and Joe go this way.

o o o

One morning, warming by the fire, we realize Brian is missing. George and I are picked to find him.

Alfred grabs my shoulder, thrusts the big knife at me. The woods are dangerous, he says.

I laugh. The woods aren't dangerous.

The woods are what's in them, he replies.

George takes the knife.

We find Brian a ways from camp. He clutches a skin pouch that holds a few slivers of smoked meat, a handful of secret nuts. His leg is caught in a metal trap.

How'd this get here? he cries.

We shrug.

I say, Where'd you get those nuts?

We unclaw his hand. The nuts tumble to the snow, and we gobble them. Our throats tighten, our stomachs buckle and twist; they're green nuts.

Help me out of this thing, Brian pleads. It hurts so much.

We look at the trap, tenderly finger its bloodied teeth.

We try to pry them. The springs tense, the hinge squawks, rust flakes. The instrument is so old, it works wrong. Or so brutal it wasn't made to ever let go. We shake our heads.

Please, I've got to get away from here. Brian's wild eyes dart to the shadowed forest, to the treetops, to us. Then he sees the knife in George's hand.

Relax, Brian. I say. You're safe.

He looks at me warily. So I smooth his hair, say, *Shh*, like a mom. His body tightens at my touch.

George begins the cut at the knee, which seems the best way through. Brian howls, gnashes, bites through the fleshiest bit of his hand, then passes out. George works the blade diligently, pausing at times to catch his breath and wipe the sweat from his forehead. The knife slips through the final connecting bridge of tendon and skin, and the lower leg plunks to the ground. I wrap the thigh to slow the bleeding, and we carry Brian back to camp—he's light like dry leaves.

The boys gather, murmur, *Poor Brian*. Brian's a boy's boy, well liked. We don't tell them how we found him, and no one asks.

Alfred says, Who's hungry?

We all are. We drank our last broth days ago.

But, Carl says.

But what?

He hasn't played the stone. So we can't—

Alfred kicks the stone over to Brian's shoulder. Brian moans from under his stupor.

Happy? Alfred sneers at Carl. None of the boys argue.

Alfred kneels by Brian, examines the stump.

Did you cut this? he asks me.

George did.

I did, George says.

Alfred eyes him. Next time, bring the rest of the leg.

But the next time, it's George who loses the game.

S oon there are just three of us: me, Alfred, Carl.

We sit around the fire, sipping broth, finishing the last of the meat. With fewer boys, we're eating so much more. I can grab and pull at my middle again. But with each meal, our appetites only grow.

I say, Perhaps we don't need to play. Winter must be ending. Couldn't we all make it to spring without more meat?

Alfred shakes his head. Spring is still very, very, very far away, he says.

I swear the world is melting. But perhaps it is a trick thaw, and we'd starve again before spring truly arrived. I wouldn't know the difference, while Alfred always seems to know. Perhaps it's best to keep playing. I'm fed and strong. If we wait and I weaken, would I feel as confident? I look at Carl. He's cracking his knuckles; he does this when weighing ideas. I always win, but Carl almost always comes in second. Alfred has never lost, yet he's only been second one time.

We agree on a race through the woods, culminating in a final set of challenges. We each place one obstacle in the field across the frozen river. Mine is a high hurdle that I know I can clear, and Carl will most likely clear, but Alfred will stumble over. Carl sets two pebbles under a massive block of ice that'll be hard for me to move, yet easy for Carl, and a breeze for Alfred. And just before the tree that will be our finish line, Alfred lays a feather.

Is that all? Carl asks.

Yes, says Alfred.

Is this a trick? I ask.

Alfred smiles and says, Just don't rustle the feather.

Now that we are clear on the rules, we begin.

o o o

I am leading, but Carl is close behind. Alfred lags farther back than normal, seemingly exhausted. At the log pile, Carl has trouble. He is gangly, while I am compact, acrobatic. I gallop ahead.

I dart sharp out of the forest and notice a bit of give in the frozen crust of the river. I bound the hurdle and smash my shoulder into the ice block, straining against it until slowly, slowly, it creaks like a glacier and I snatch a pebble. I tiptoe in a wide loop around the feather, my eyes fixed on it, terrified a breeze will disturb it. *Is* this a trick? But there is no wind, and nothing happens. I've won.

I hug the tree and cry a little, and I have this tingling feeling, like this is how it feels to be eleven.

o o o

The sun lowers. The air freezes. I've been waiting a long time for Carl and Alfred to appear.

I return to camp and build a fire. My stomach gnaws itself. I fall asleep. When I wake, Alfred is at the edge of the clearing, carrying a limp Carl. Blood dapples the snow as they approach.

What happened? I ask.

Alfred lays him by the fire and sits. Carl curls in on himself. A split on his forehead oozes, his foot points in the opposite direction from his knee.

I found him a bit past the log pile, Alfred says. He must have tripped.

Carl quivers in his ball.

I don't know what to do, Alfred says, sucking on some of the new bloodstained snow. I was losing until Carl fell. But after that, he obviously wouldn't have finished. If I'd left him, he'd be the one to go. I carried him back here instead, and so in a way we've finished at the same time.

We don't have a rule for this, Alfred continues. And we're hungry. He stretches. I'm very perplexed, he says, though his voice is flat and does not sound perplexed at all. I'll fetch water.

When he's gone, I scoot toward Carl. What happened? I ask him.

I ran into a log.

You didn't see it?

It wasn't there to be seen. It swung out of nowhere.

I made it through fine, I say skeptically.

I know.

Do you think it was a trick?

Don't you?

But he carried you out.

I know. I know. Carl bites his lip, glances around the camp. He leans closer and whispers, We need to stop playing these games right now.

I'm quiet for a minute, then say, It was nice of Alfred to

help you. He didn't have to. If we had a rule for what's happened, I think that rule would say that you lost. I think it's only fair to look at this as your loss. If there were any boys left, I know they'd agree.

Carl's mouth gapes open, hollow like a stomach.

Just then, Alfred returns with the water, and a crown of dead grass and baked mud that must have taken him a few days to make.

Between Carl and me sits the stone. As we'd whispered, we'd each unknowingly rested a hand on it. I slowly slide mine off.

Carl, you're playing the stone? I exclaim.

He looks at his hand, then at me, rolly-eyed.

Oh, Alfred says, like he's surprised. He presents the pebble, plucked from under Carl's ice obstacle. It is a speckled, mineral white. I was going to give this to you, for you to win, he says to Carl, who jerks his hand from the stone like he has been burned. But you know the rules. Once you play the stone . . .

Carl sputters and squeals and claws at the frozen earth, trying to drag himself away.

Alfred picks up the stone. It looks small in his meaty hands, but dead-dropped, it will crush a boy.

o o o

The days grow longer, and wherever we step, water squishes and pools. The river groans as planes of ice break apart and slide over it. The breeze carries the mustiness of freed pollen, mud, green things. I *know* spring is near. But still the world freezes deeply each night while we sleep, and we wake dusted with snow, and nothing stirs but the wind and the trees and me and Alfred.

One cold dawn Alfred eyes me.

I'm hungry, he says. It's just us.

We still have bones about, I say, getting the pot ready for boiling. I can make a broth.

I'm not hungry for broth, he says flatly.

Well, soon we'll be able to hunt. I can feel it. I can hear the thaw. Yesterday morning I heard seven kinds of warbler. And the river is beginning to run again. Have you noticed? In the gaps between the ice, it looks like black silk rippling. I would have kept talking nonsense forever to get him to stop eyeing me.

But I'm hungry now.

I can wait, I say. I can wait for spring.

He stretches out his arms—they are veined and muscled—and yawns, bleary-eyed, bored. What shall we play?

I don't answer.

Alfred smiles. I'm partial to tag. I'll be the tagger first.

What are the rules?

When I tag you, I win.

But how do I win?

You don't get tagged. Alfred strains to rise, as if he's having trouble in his own body. But once standing, he seems taller, stouter than before.

Of course, I had imagined this moment coming. With just two of us left, we could become partners, brothers, or we could carry on as we had.

I don't have time or choice; I run. I am nimbler. I tell myself I can keep ahead. I always have.

Behind me his footfalls are like the cracks of an ax against a tree, chopping it down.

We run for a long time, deep into the forest, then loop back around. I glance continually over my shoulder, expecting him to be far back, but he's always right behind me.

We're evenly matched, I yell, though I have always easily beaten him. Perhaps we should call a truce.

No, Alfred yells.

We splash mud everywhere. I feel the warmth release from it. With every breath I smell green.

Why are we running? I yell again. It's so clearly spring. I'm running past the shoots of new plants piercing the snow, seeking the sun. They *know*.

I'm running because you're running, Alfred says.

If you stop chasing me, I'll dig up some bulbs and make us a hearty soup.

Alfred growls, I don't want bulb soup.

We continue all day and through the night. I tear small branches as I go, gnaw them and suck their green, bitter sugar. I'm not sure I can carry on. But then I carry on.

As dawn breaks, I can't feel my legs. When I don't think I can take another step, I yell, I'll make you a deal. I'll find all your food for you. I'll do everything. Just stop chasing me.

You'll fail.

I won't fail, because in the end I always have myself to give. If I can't provide, I'll be the meal.

We are thumping along the river, which now runs swift, the ice sheets breached over rocks. The rising sun turns the black world blue. I don't hear his breath so harsh behind me anymore, but I feel a new chill, like his hands are right at my neck.

And that's when I hear shouting, laughter, commotion far off. I am stunned, forget everything and stop. Alfred whizzes right by me through the thicket and disappears into the trees.

I hear his unmistakable voice, familiar and clear, like a brother among the stranger tones, the high and light calls of boys newly spit from the Chute: This way! A camp! I've found a camp!

The ruckus quickens and moves, whipped to action. I circle back and slip quietly into the clearing just as the boys tumble in and their eyes adjust; they are truly seeing one another for the first time.

I clear my throat, feign wonder: Do you think we're the first boys to escape the Chute?

We can't be, a small boy insists.

We must be, Alfred says. Otherwise there would be a whole community here of boys like us. But older.

This is when the boys understand that they're here for good. They get quiet, excited, scared.

Above their heads the sun crests the dark trees, and Alfred smiles at me through the flickery orange light.

ACKNOWLEDGMENTS

Thanks and gratitude:

For early and late reads, edits, inspiring actions, advice, excitement, or just in general: Karolina Waclawiak, Jonathan Goldstein, Alissa Shipp, Lisa Pollak, Starlee Kine, Ira Glass, Julie Snyder, Jane Marie, Sarah Jetzon, Anjali Goswami, Jamie York, Rebecca Wright, Aric Knuth, Laura Wetherington, Hannah Ensor, Rachael Cohen, the Just Family, Don Cook, Ramon Isao, Megan Lynch, Emily Miller, Cheryl Tan, Daniel Pipski, Heidi Julavits. Special thanks to Sam Lipsyte, Rebecca Curtis, Ben Marcus, and the excellent members of their workshops at Columbia, who saw early drafts of a few of these stories and were always encouraging, excitable, sharp. Biggest thanks to my Writing Group for all the reasons above and more: Jessamine Chan, Yael Korman, Hilary Leichter, Heather Monley, Mary South, and Lee Ellis (emeritus): Writing Group!

For time, space, support, community: Yaddo, the Albee Foundation, the Vermont Studio Center. Special gratitude to the Sitka Center for Art and Ecology, where I plumbed the big ideas and inspirations that shaped this book.

For journal encouragement, inclusion, and making-it-better edits: Meakin Armstrong, Cathy Chung, Case Kerns,

Annie Liontas, Christopher Cox, Michael Ray, Rob Spillman, Meg Storey, Sigrid Rausing. Thanks to the University of Louisville Creative Writing program and Rick Simmons for championing the Calvino Prize.

To the New England Literature Program staff and students for helping me build foundations under these air castles.

To my agent, Seth Fishman, for guidance, enthusiasm, and wisdom. To my editor, Terry Karten, for soulful reads and patience. And to the entire hardworking Harper team.

To my dad for being encouraging, skeptical, and awestruck at the right times.

And to Jorge Just, my first reader, best friend, and love, until the end of the world.

**A daring and imaginative debut novel about a mother's
battle to save her daughter in a world on the brink**

Bea's five-year-old daughter, Agnes, is wasting away, ravaged by the
smog and pollution of the overdeveloped, overpopulated metropolis
they call home. Bea knows she cannot stay in the city, but there is
only one alternative: The Wilderness State. Mankind has never
ventured into this vast expanse of untamed land. Until now.

Somewhere between a science experiment and refugees, Bea and
Agnes slowly learn how to live in this unpredictable, often dangerous
land. But as Agnes embraces the radical freedom of this new
existence, Bea realises that saving her daughter's life might mean
losing her in a different way.

At once a blazing lament of our contempt for nature and a deeply
humane portrayal of motherhood, *The New Wilderness* is an
extraordinary, urgent novel.

'Gut-wrenching and heart-wrecking, this is a book that demands to
be read.'
Rachel Khong, author of *Goodbye, Vitamin*

'This is not just a thrilling, curious, vibrant book—but an essential
one.'
Alexandra Kleeman,
author of *You Too Can Have a Body Like Mine*

Read on for a sample of *The New Wilderness*,
the astounding debut novel from Diane Cook

THE BABY EMERGED from Bea the color of a bruise. Bea burned the cord somewhere between them and uncoiled it from the girl's slight neck and, though she knew it was useless, swept her daughter up into her hands, tapped on her soft chest, and blew a few shallow breaths into her slimy mouth.

Around her, the singular song of crickets expanded. Bea's skin prickled from heat. Sweat dried on her back and face. The sun had crested and would, more quickly than seemed right, fall again. From where Bea knelt, she saw their Valley, its secret grasses and sage. In the distance were plopped lonely buttes and, closer, mud mounds that looked like cairns marking the way somewhere. The Caldera stood sharp and white on the horizon.

Bea dug into the hard earth with a stick, then a stone, then hollowed and smoothed it with her hands. She scooped the placenta into it. Then the girl. The hole was shallow and her baby's belly jutted from it. Wet from birth, the little body held onto coarse sand and tiny golden buds brittled from their stems by the heat of the sun. She sprinkled more dust onto the baby's forehead, pulled from her deerhide bag several wilted green leaves, and laid them over the girl. She broke off craggy branches from the surrounding sage, laid them over the distended belly, the absurdly small shoulders. The baby was a misshapen mound of plant green, rust-red blood, a dull violet map of veins under wet tissue skin.

Now, the animals, who had sensed it, were converging. In the sky, a cyclone of buzzards lowered as if to check on the progress, then uplifted on a thermal. She heard the soft tread of coyotes. They wove through the bloomy sage. A mother and three skinny kits appeared under jaggedly thrown shade. Bea heard whines ease from their impassive yawns. They would wait.

A wind stirred and she breathed in the dusty heat. She missed the stagnant scent of the hospital room where she'd given birth to Agnes what must have been eight years ago now. The way the scratchy gown had stretched across her chest and gotten tangled up when she tried to roll to either side. How the cool air blew around her hips, between her legs, where her doctor and nurses stared, prodded, and pulled Agnes from her. She'd hated the feeling. So exposed, used, animal-like. But here, it was all dust and hot air. Here, she had needed to guide the small body—five months old? Six? Seven?—out with one hand while with the other she'd had to block a diving magpie. She had wanted to be alone for this. But what she wouldn't have given for a probing gloved hand, stale recirculated air, humming machines, fresh sheets under her rather than desert dust. Some sterile comfort.

What she wouldn't have given for her mother.

Bea hissed at the coyotes. "Scram," she said, pitching the dirt and pebbles she'd just dug at them. But they only slid their ears back, the mother sinking to her haunches and the kits nipping at her snout, irritating her. She probably snuck off from the rest of the pack to get her young something extra, or to let them practice scavenging, to practice surviving. It's what mothers did.

Bea shooed a fly from near the baby's eyes, which at first had looked startled over having not made it, but now seemed accusatory. The truth was Bea hadn't wanted the baby. Not here. It would have been wrong to bring her into this world. That's what she'd felt all along. But what if the girl had sensed Bea's dread and died from not being wanted?

Bea choked. "This is for the best," she told her. The girl's eyes clouded over with the clouds that rolled overhead.

During one nightwalk, back when she'd had a flashlight and still carried batteries to make it glow, she'd caught two eyes gleaming in her beam. She clapped her hands to scare the eyes, but they just dipped down. The animal was tall but crouching, sitting perhaps, and Bea feared it was stalking her. Her heart sped up and she waited for the cold dread that she'd felt a couple of times by then. Her inner sense of being in danger. But the feeling never came. She walked closer. Again the eyes dipped down, supplicant, like a dog obeying, but it was not a dog. She had to get closer before she could see that it was a deer with its sloped back, the peaked ears, the resigned flick of the tail. Then Bea saw another eye in the light, small, not looking at her, but quivering, unsteady. The deer heaved up and then the quivering eye wobbled up too. It was a small glistening fawn, on shaky, toothpick legs. Bea had unknowingly witnessed a birth. Quiet in the dark. Bea had come stealthily upon the mother like a predator. And the mother could do nothing in that moment but lower her head as though asking to be spared.

There were few things Bea let herself regret these days, these unpredictable days full of survival so plain and brute. But she wished she had walked another way that night, not found their eyes in her light, so that the doe could have had her birth, nuzzled and licked her baby clean, could have had the chance to give her baby a first unblemished night before the work of survival began. Instead the doe lumbered away, exhausted, the fawn stumbling after her, disoriented, and that was the beginning of their life together. It's why, days ago, when Bea no longer felt the kicks and hiccups and flutters and knew the baby had died, she knew she'd want to be alone for the birth. It was the only moment they would have together. She did not want to share that. She did not want someone watching her own complicated version of grief.

Bea peered at the coyote mother. "You understand, don't you?"

The coyote pranced impatiently and licked her yellow teeth.

From a far low ridge, some foothills of foothills to come, she heard a joyless howl; some watching wolf had seen the carrion birds, was signaling prey.

She had to leave. The sun was going. And now the wolves knew. She'd tracked her shadow becoming long and thin, a sight that always made her sad, as though she were seeing her own death by starvation. She stood, stretched out her sand-pocked knees, wiped the desert off her skin and ragged tunic. She felt foolish that she'd tried to resuscitate what she knew to be dead. She thought the Wilderness had cast all sentimentality from her. She would not tell anyone about that moment. Not Glen, who she thought wanted a child of his own more than he would ever admit. She wouldn't tell Agnes, even though she thought Agnes would want to know about this sister who never materialized, would want to understand the secret particulars of her mother. No, she would stick to the simple story. The baby did not survive. So many others hadn't. So we move on.

She turned without another look at this girl she had wanted to name Madeline. She gave that mother coyote another sharp kick, landing it against her visible ribs. The dog yelped, slunk, then snarled, but she had more pressing concerns than engaging a human insult.

Bea heard the scuffle and yips behind her. And though the dogs' rising excitement resembled a newborn's cry, Bea knew it was just the sound of hunger.

* * *

AN UNMISTAKABLE SHADOW of a path led toward the camp. It was hard to know if it was from the Community's own impact, animals making their own animal trails, or a remnant of all the things the land had been before it became the Wilderness State. Maybe it was Bea alone who had blazed the trail. She visited that place as often as she could, whenever they migrated through the Valley. It was the reason she'd chosen it for Madeline. There was something subtle in that view. It seemed like a hidden valley. The depression of verdant grasses and coarse bushes lay slightly lower than the land around it so that it had a secret view toward the horizon and the inky hump of mountains there. All the land in view formed a mosaic of blurred, muted colors. It was pretty and quiet and private, she thought. A place someone wouldn't want to leave. Again, Bea felt a fleeting relief to have Madeline poised there, instead of facing an unknowable landscape with her, a mother who felt incapable of maneuvering it with grace.

Bea could hear the voices of the others in camp. They carried across the even, empty land and dropped at her feet. But she did not want to return to them and their questions or, possibly worse, their silence. She shifted away and scrambled up boulders toward the shallow cave where her family liked to spend time. Their secret perch. She saw her husband, Glen, and daughter, Agnes, above her, kneeling in the dirt, waiting for her.

Bea saw Glen's brow furrowing in concentration as he spun a leaf by its stem, peering at it from every vantage, pointing to something on its green spine so Agnes could see, asking her to notice some remarkable detail in its common shape. They both leaned closer to the leaf, as though it were telling them its secret, their faces breaking into delight.

When Glen saw her approaching, he waved her toward them. Agnes did the same, a generous and awkward sweep of her arm, smiling with her newly jagged tooth, chipped against a boulder. *Why couldn't it have been a baby tooth?* Bea had thought, her daughter's head in her hands, inspecting the damage under her bright, bloody lip. Agnes had held still and quiet, one tear squeezing from her eye and trailing through the dirt on her face. It was the only way Bea knew the accident had fazed her. Like an animal, Agnes froze when fearful and bolted when endangered. Bea imagined that as Agnes grew up this would change. She might feel less like prey and more like a predator. It was something in her daughter's smile, some unnameable knowledge. It was the smile of a girl biding her time.

"This one is alder," Glen was saying when Bea reached them. He took her hand, kissed it gently, lingering until she pulled it back to her side. She saw him glance at her stomach and wince.

He had prepared hot water in the brutish wood bowl, but now it was the temperature of the air. She squatted next to them, lifted her tunic, spread her knees. She scooped water under her skirt and gently washed between her legs, her stretched, worn folds, her splattered thighs. It was raw, but she could tell she had not torn.

Agnes assumed the same position, her slight and toady legs splayed, splashing imaginary water on herself, eyeing Bea carefully. She seemed intent on not looking at where the baby had been.

Agnes was in some kind of mimicry stage. Bea saw it in animals. She'd seen it in other children. But in Agnes something about it disarmed her. She'd understood Agnes up until recently. Around the time the leaves last turned color, Agnes had become strange to her. She didn't know if this fissure was just something parents went through with their children, or mothers went through with daughters, or if it was just some special hardship she and Agnes would have to endure. Out here, it was hard for Bea to dismiss things as simply normal because every aspect of their lives here was anything but normal. Was Agnes behaving normally for her age, or was it possible she believed she was a wolf?

Agnes had just turned eight but didn't know it. They no longer marked birthdays because they no longer marked days. But Bea had taken notice of certain blooms when they'd first arrived. Then, Agnes had just turned five years old. It was April on the calendar. Bea had noted a field of violets during their first several days of walking. When she saw violets again, it seemed likely a year had passed— they'd felt the heat of summer, they'd seen leaves turn color, and they'd shivered in the snowy mountains. The snow had gone. She'd seen violets four times. Four birthdays. She knew Agnes's eighth birthday had happened sometime since the last full moon, when she had seen violets in a patch of grass near their last camp. When they'd first arrived, Agnes had been so gravely ill, Bea hadn't been sure she would see violets again with her daughter. But there they were, Agnes bounding through them.

Bea crept toward the back of the shallow cave. From behind a boulder, in a divot she'd hollowed out on their first time making camp here, she pulled a throw pillow and a design and architecture magazine that had featured one of her decorating remodels. It was a national magazine and the spread had been a turning point in her career, though not long after it published, she left for the Wilderness. These were her secret treasures she'd smuggled in from the City, and rather than carry them place to place, facing scorn from the others and damage from the elements, she hid them, blatantly disregarding the rules laid out in the Manual. When they passed through the Valley, which they had a few times each year, she dug out her treasures so she could feel a little more like herself.

She sat next to Glen and hugged her pillow. Then she thumbed through the pages of her spread, remembering the choices she'd made and why. Remembering what it felt like to have a home.

"If the Rangers find those, we'll get in trouble," Glen said, as he always said when she dug out her treasures, always so concerned with the rules.

She scowled. "What are they going to do? Kick us out for a pillow?"

"Maybe." Glen shrugged.

"Relax," she said. "They'll never find them. And I need them. I need to remember what pillows are like."

"Aren't I a good enough pillow?" He said this so sweetly.

Bea looked at him. He was all bones. They both were. Even her belly, which had barely jutted with the baby, seemed to have immediately sunken. When she looked up at him, he was offering a small broken smile. She nodded. He nodded back. Then he staged a long, loud, languid yawn, eyeing Agnes. Agnes's yawn followed with a big, fisted stretch.

"Big day tomorrow," he said. "We start our trip to Middle Post. And we get to cross your favorite river on the way."

"Can we swim?" Agnes asked.

"We've got to get in it to cross it, so you bet."

"When?"

"Probably be there in a few days."

"How much is a few?"

Glen shrugged. "Five? Ten? Several?"

Agnes huffed. "That's not an answer!"

Glen poked her and laughed. "We'll get there when we get there."
Agnes's scowl was just like Bea's scowl.

"Is everything packed?" Bea asked.

"Mostly. You don't have to worry."

Bea gave the pillow in her lap a tight squeeze. It was moist and
smelled bitter, but she didn't care. She buried her face and squeezed,
imagining she could transfer love to her small baby. She sighed and
looked up.

Agnes was watching her, hugging the air, pretending to have her
own pillow, or perhaps her own baby, and smiling the same sad smile
Bea had no doubt just displayed.

The bustling and hoot-filled evening quieted as they passed
through it.

At camp, a few of the other Community members were still at
the fire, but most were breathing lightly in the circle where everyone slept. Bea and Glen eased down under the elk pelt they used as
bedding. Agnes arranged herself, as she always did, at their feet. Her
hand curled around Bea's ankle like a vine.

"Maybe there will be some good packages at Post," Glen murmured. "Maybe some good chocolate or something like that."

Bea *hmm*ed, but really she couldn't eat things like that anymore
without becoming ill, her body overwhelmed by what it used to
crave in their old life.

Instead of chocolate, she wished instead Glen would mention the
child she'd just buried. Or she thought she wished for that. What
would she say? What could she say that he didn't already know? And

did she really want to talk about it? No, she didn't. And he knew that too.

She looked at Glen, and in the firelight saw a look of hope play on his face. He knew chocolate couldn't soothe such bewilderment, but maybe the suggestion could do what the chocolate was supposed to. She fit herself into his arms. "Yes, some chocolate would be nice," she lied.

All around them, Bea heard the sounds of the wild world bedding down. Ground owls cooed, and something else screeched; shadows of night fliers skimmed between the sky and the stars. As the campfire hissed itself to sleep, she heard the last of the Community walking cautious and blind from the fire to the beds and nestling down. Someone said, "Good night, everyone."

Against her ankle, Bea could feel Agnes's blood pulsing through her hot clutching hand. She breathed in and out to its rhythm, and it focused her. *I have a daughter,* she thought, *and no time for brooding.* She was needed here, and now, by someone. She vowed to move on quickly. She wanted to. She had to. It was how they lived now.